THE BORNLESS KEEPER

Dedicated to Harriet, a faithful secretary

P. B. Yuill

The Bornless
Keeper

Futura Publications Limited

A Futura Book

First published in Great Britain in 1974
by Macmillan London Limited
First Futura Publications edition 1975

ISBN 0 8600 71510
Printed in Great Britain by
C. Nicholls & Company Ltd
The Philips Park Press
Manchester

Futura Publications Limited
49 Poland Street
LONDON W1A 2LG

CHAPTER ONE

The grotesque feathered head cocked this way and that, watching and listening. Something was wrong.

A delicate breeze whispered and sighed through the tops of the huge silver firs; down here the secret, teeming life of Peacock Island lay slumbering in the heavy afternoon heat.

Under a gloomy awning of rhododendron leaves the feathered silhouette remained motionless. For a moment the silence was broken by the chatter of bickering jays somewhere in the dense woods.

The deep-set eyes moved slowly, scanning every inch of the castle and its surrounds. Nothing moved. Not a blade of grass stirred on the slope of long-neglected lawn that led down to the grey castle walls. Not a sound came from the leaded windows.

Yet something was wrong.

Toes moved silently on black earth. Then a dazzle of blue feathers streaked from the massive bushes, down the slope, crouching momentarily behind a twisted apple tree, then darting to the shelter of a sunless wall.

Hidden among the tall weeds and brambles that licked like green fire at the castle's foundations, the feathered head waited for signs of danger. Giant bumble-bees droned past the dark sockets of the large brown eyes. Tiny orchestras of grasshoppers scraped endlessly in the long grass.

For a moment the high August sun glinted on lustrous blue feathers and then there was the creaking of a heavy door, the soft slap of tough skin on cold flagstones. Delicate nostrils sniffed—and the feathered shape froze.

Amid the familiar mustiness of the disused kitchens there was a new odour. But still there was no other movement or sound in the castle's gloomy interior.

The feathered creature moved into the faintly lit vault of the great hall. Up the stairway, the air as dry and stale as the inside of a time-forgotten tomb. The new smell was stronger here.

From shadow to shadow moved the squat, feathered shape, its gaudy hues now dark tints against cracked panelling and mouldering fabrics.

A low corridor, no sound coming now from the tough-skinned feet. Into the ghostly light of the bed-room, a single ray of dust-clouded sunshine cutting down through unfathomable shadows. The sudden crack of a dry floorboard, then a pattering noise, a light scuttling, a faint hubbub of feverish squeaking, a rush of dark shapes scurrying for the shadows, delicate claws sliding and scraping on oak, a shaking and shivering of vast dust-sheets.

The stench of old decay and vermin mingled with something newer and more sickly.

The massive bird-shape moved towards the canopied bed. The profile of the head on the sepia pillow was on a level with the dark eye-sockets of the feathered face. Silver hair outlined a partially sculpted skull, gaping nose-holes in a faintly greenish glow of phosphorescence.

For a moment the feathered creature froze. Then, terror obvious in every movement, the feet slithered and slapped along the low corridor and down the great stair-way, through the stone-flagged kitchens.

A dart of brilliant peacock blue zig-zagged up the sunny slope and disappeared into the sunless under-world of the island's secret ways. A branch quivered, its leaves shook for a second, then there was only the riffle of the treetop breeze and the muffled drilling of a woodpecker.

Back in the silent bedroom on the first floor of the castle tiny noses twitched as the greedy tribe of rats tested the air for danger and then prepared to resume their interrupted feast.

CHAPTER TWO

As soon as the last passenger had been helped down off Gallow Quay into the well of the *Mundham Queen* Turle Greeno put the diesel into reverse while his brother Jack and the boy pulled in the trailing ropes. With the crowds and the cars falling behind Turle Greeno opened the throttle and the seated rows of holidaymakers felt a breeze off the glinting waters of the vast, landlocked harbour.

By the time Turle had steered the converted fishing-boat through the Town Yacht Club moorings and set her slightly starboard for Dog Buoy, Jack and the boy had collected the fares.

'We'll make Castle Quay about full tide this trip,' Turle said, holding the wheel until Jack had stowed the cash away and could take over the steering. 'We'll manage three more trips 'fore we pack up, eh?'

'Four if we go quick,' said Jack.

It was a short season and in two weeks it would be September, when the queues for trips round the harbour would shorten and then disappear. Sixty passengers at twenty-five pence a head was profitable enough but the money had to be made in a very short time. Every winter the fishing became poorer and

Mundham boats were having to go farther out into the English Channel to find the sprat shoals.

Some blamed it on pollution, some on over-fishing. Soon there might not be a living in fishing. To the fishermen the holiday trade became more important each year, only silly little trips round the harbour's islands but Turle Greeno was no romantic. He picked up the battery-powered megaphone.

'Good afternoon,' he began, 'glad to have you on board. Now, if you look ahead to the right you'll see Peacock Island—we can't approach it direct 'cause of the mud banks.'

The *Mundham Queen*'s passengers twisted round on two rows of slatted bench seats. Jack Greeno steered well clear of the starting line of a yacht club dinghy race. For a moment or so they were within a few yards of the becalmed flotilla of triangular sails, most of them in the new fashion, reds, broad blue stripes on yellow, even one with a floral pattern.

The yachtsmen affected to ignore the holidaymakers, who focused their cameras or let their hands dangle over the sides in water that was a sparkling, opaque green. An irritable mother shook a small boy who announced, loudly, that he wanted to go wee-wees. Turle raised the loudhailer.

'The first records of Peacock Island—it had some other name then—show it belonged to the Abbot of Trevis, about fifty years before William the Conqueror landed at Hastings. There's supposed to have been ancient people on it before that—if you look up the top end you'll see where the trees are taller—them that study these things say that was a sacred place for the ancient Britons ... that's the sacred dell mentioned in the curse of Peacock Island.'

Faces turned expectantly.

'Oh yes,' said Turle, injecting a well-practised note

of melodrama into his battery-amplified voice, 'the island has its curse and not a very pretty one either.'

'Nice place for a picnic,' said a stout woman in a Birmingham accent.

'I'm afraid you're out of luck, missus,' said Turle. 'The owner, Lady Bennett, is very keen on her privacy, nobody is allowed on the island, nobody at all.'

They were now passing along the north shore. Turle told them that the heavily-wooded island was a mile and a half long and half a mile wide.

The passengers were waiting to hear more about the legend of the curse but Turle always saved the best for last. It helped the tips.

'You might think it looks easy enough to land on that little shingle beach,' he went on, 'but between us and there is mud, only about eighteen inches of water even at high tide. Lots of visiting boats get caught on them banks. You won't find any locals trying it. The island's always had a bad name among Mundham folk. The Vikings used it as a base for their expeditions inland— they'd bring their loot and captured women back here —then the Romans had a camp on it, there's what's said to be an authentic Roman bath still there among the trees somewhere.'

The *Mundham Queen*, still carrying her brass plate to show she had been to Dunkirk, left a wide arc of frothy wake as Jack took her round the north-west corner and then past a skeleton of rotting piles, all that re-mained of the old clayworks jetty. Turle put the mega-phone down for a quick pull at a bottle of lemonade. People stood up to take snaps. Turle lit a cigarette, care-fully replacing the match in the box. He saw a woman drop a crumple of paper wrappings over the edge. Somebody else lobbed an empty Coca-Cola can clear of the rippling bow-wave. He shrugged. It was only what you expected of people these days.

Coming down the thick, coffin-shaped mass of land covered by trees and dense greenery he told them about the crumbling ruins of the old clayworks, the claypool in the middle, the ornamental gardens stocked with exotic plants from all over the world by the wealthy people through whose hands the island's title-deeds had passed since the dissolution of the monasteries, when Henry the Eighth had granted Peacock Island to a court favourite.

Then they came past a high sweep of sheer cliffs, the rocky base lapped by harbour water, the top overgrown with bushes and banks of creeping blackberry.

'Now then, the curse,' he said, smiling slightly, a murmur passing down the lines of passengers, a base-ball-capped father telling his young son to take the transistor away from his ear and listen to the commentary. 'The legend says the island has a guardian spirit, it's called the Bornless Keeper—bornless, like the Devil, not born the way we know—he's supposed to drive off intruders. He's done a good job over the centuries. The old histories say the Vikings went down in a storm just out in the sea past Monks Sweep—then there was the time the only inhabitant was a hermit, a religious man, he was given the wreckin' rights by the Abbot. You heard of wreckers? They were too greedy to wait for the sea to do the work, they put up lanterns in the wrong places. Gallow Quay now, it got its name from days when anybody due for hangin' in Mundham was brought out here and strung up in front of the castle. There was about three hundred people lived on the island when the clayworks was operatin', that was another tragedy, the claypits went broke, the people were all bein' taken off, they must have overloaded one of the boats with furniture and stuff, it turned over in the main channel, funny thing, it was all men and boys on board, nine of them, drowned with their womenfolk

12

watchin' and helpless—you see out there where the water gets choppier? That's the main channel, comes from the sea through Monks Sweep and round to the town quays, a very fast current when the tide's goin' out, I never heard of anybody bein' able to swim it. Now, you can see the castle and the cottages there, where the servants and boatmen used to live—this is as close as we're allowed to go, Lady Bennett is very strict about trespassin'. You may be interested to know I'm the boatman who takes her what she needs, paraffin, tins of stuff and bread and suchlike, just once a fortnight or so, and I'm only allowed on the end of the quay, I hardly ever see her lately. As a boy I can remember when the Bennetts were first come to the island, they had parties and balls in the castle, lights all over the battlements, rich people comin' all the way from London—Sir Godfrey died towards the end of the war—and then came the last tragedy connected with Peacock—about twelve year ago, Lady Bennett had some buildin' work she wanted doin', three builders, Irish chaps, were on the island for about a fortnight; one day I was bringin' them over some crates of ale and stuff and they said the job was almost done, I asked if they wanted me to pick 'em up but they didn't need transport, they said, the old lady was givin' them a present of her own boat, she didn't use it since her old boatman retired, they were goin' to sail it over to the town and sell it. I warned them about the currents and the mud banks but they were big strong lads, they could manage, they said.'

He paused. Sixty faces, less those of the smaller children playing among the grown-up knees, stared at him intently.

'They never did reach the town. They sank just over there, a bit past those two cabin-cruisers. The bodies turned up in a day or so, one was caught in the current and taken out through Monks Sweep, my brother Jack here and me pulled another out of the harbour.'

Jack began to turn the *Mundham Queen* back into the main channel. The passengers stared wonderingly at the castle and the treacherously calm waters. The little cluster of grey stone cottages that lay between the island's quay and the castle fell astern. Turle lifted the megaphone:

'This is what the curse says: *Tread ye on this sacred dell the Bornless Keeper ye shall see, pointing the road to Hell.*'

He winked. Some of the faces smiled.

'Thank you, ladies and gentlemen, we'll be back at Gallow Quay in ten minutes. I hope you enjoyed the trip and my little commentary effort.'

A few passengers applauded. The boy went among the passengers with a wooden-handled church collection bag into which they were perfectly at liberty to drop a small appreciation of their guide's performance. Turle tapped Jack on the shoulder.

'You see what I saw on the jetty, Jack?'

Jack shook his head, concentrating on avoiding the oncoming line of three flat-bottomed power-boats zipping and bucking for Monks Sweep and the sea.

'The bag is still under the seat, she hasn't been down for it,' said Turle.

'When did you leave it?'

'Thursday, she's never left it that long.'

'Somethin' wrong, you reckon?'

'Could be ill.'

'Serves her right, livin' there on her own, no phone or anythin', stands to reason she could have a heart attack or anythin', who's to know? What're you goin' to do, then?'

'Dunno.' Turle frowned, eyes peering back over the heads of the passengers at the receding island. 'I could land and see if there's somethin' wrong but you know what she's like.'

'She can't do nothin' to you.'

'I know that.'

'What you scared of, then? The dog's been dead three year.'

'Look, all them visitors and yachtsmen see me landin' in broad daylight? Give them ideas, won't it? Only us know she don't have a guard dog any more.'

'Wouldn't be a bad thing if she were gone at last,' said Jack sourly. 'Time that island was opened up to the public, be a big attraction.'

'I could make a special trip in the mornin' early,' said Turle.

'Suit yourself,' Jack growled, turning the wheel with a strong brown hand as he moved the *Mundham Queen* farther out towards the yacht club moorings to avoid a tramp coaster that had just delivered a cargo of artificial fertiliser to the town quay, its black hull and grimy superstructure moving incongruously through yacht sails and white motor-cruisers.

'No, I'd better have a look, next time out you can drop me at the castle jetty, if she's ill it wouldn't be right to leave her alone another night.'

'It's up to you,' said Jack, adding with a slight note of bitterness, 'it's you she gives the fivers to, after all.'

As soon as the boat eased alongside Gallow Quay Jack said he was going to make a phone call about a second-hand car.

'Don't be long,' said Turle, helping some children across the steep drop between the side of the boat and the quay.

Jack hurried through the crowds of holidaymakers, almost running when he saw that one of the phone boxes beside the public lavatory was unoccupied. He dialled a nine-digit number starting with 01, the London code

When the clicks started he shoved a tenpenny piece in the slot.

'Artel Productions,' said the girl's voice.

'Mister Maltravers,' Jack grunted, adding quickly, 'if you keep me hangin' about I shall ring off and there won't be no boat for him.'

It was not easy to get the languid Julian Maltravers to show anger but Victoria Dryden-Chambers, a red-haired woman in a blue shirt and white trouser suit, was succeeding, to her intense satisfaction.

'You had no right to sack Darcy,' Maltravers snapped. 'You just didn't like him and you waited till I was away from the office—'

'Be fair, Julian,' said Abendsohn, the man the merchant bank had put in to safeguard its investment, 'we agreed there had to be a twenty-per-cent cut in over-heads, Darcy was costing almost five thousand a year and—'

'Cheap for a good staff cameraman,' Maltravers said abruptly. 'You ever tried to get a reliable freelance at the last moment for some rush job?'

Victoria Dryden-Chambers tapped her cigarette against the inner rim of the Wedgwood ashtray.

'It was exactly those rush jobs that got us into this financial morass,' she said. 'From now on we're going to look very hard indeed at any of these last-minute schemes. They—'

'They made us one of the best-known small independents in the television business,' Maltravers said. 'If we sit round on our backsides waiting for sure-fire guaranteed profits we'll be dead in six months. Our whole strength against the big networks is to be quick and imaginative and flexible—'

'I agree entirely,' said Victoria, smiling at Abend-sohn. 'Perhaps that's why our new masters were imagi-

16

native enough to put their trust in a mere female.'

'Oh God,' Maltravers drawled. 'Hasn't control got that boring old chip off your shoulder?'

'Can we get on with the actual business?' said Tewson, head of the cutting rooms. 'I've got that Lake District stuff to edit besides—'.

'Right,' said Victoria, picking up the photostatted list of possible projects. 'I suggest scrubbing that thing on the Kent miners, can't see any foreign sales there—' Maltravers shrugged—'and unless anyone has a better angle I'm also for scrubbing this idea about imported Philippino textile workers, I saw them on the BBC, they're not svelte Asian beauties by any means—'

'Spoken just like a man,' said Maltravers airily. The mood of the meeting was not on his side and he was realising that Victoria was cleverer than he'd given her credit for.

'—and Julian, what were you thinking about with this island story of yours? Sounds like a boring old travelogue. Peacocks and trees—so what?'

'It's a good yarn,' he said, determined now not to look as though she was needling him, 'mysterious island paradise owned by rich old recluse who lives entirely on her own, rich in historical anecdote, a Roman bath, I used to go there a bit, *very* visual—'

'Wordy,' she said, almost brutally. 'Exactly the kind of job we used to think up to keep Darcy occupied.'

Maltravers made a half-hearted attempt to defend the story. It would make a nice half-hour colour feature that would probably repay its costs from a British network sale, leaving syndication in America, Australia, Germany and elsewhere as profit.

'Dribs and drabs,' said Victoria dismissively.

The phone rang, the only one on the long mahogany table. It was in front of Victoria.

'I said no calls,' she snapped. Then she handed it

17

across the table to Maltravers. 'Long-distance for you, she says it sounds urgent.'

'I'll take it outside. Don't sack anybody until I get back.'

When he had left the smoke-hazed room Abendsohn said:

'We don't necessarily have to be too drastic, not at first, Victoria.'

'On the contrary.' Her voice was now a little hoarse. There were no windows in the board-room, which was a plasterboard construction recently installed in the middle of the company's third-floor Soho offices. 'Those breakdowns of last year's figures—'

Maltravers came back into the room and slid into his chair.

'Sorry about that,' he said. 'Coincidentally, it was a call about Peacock Island. Now, where were we?'

'What about Peacock Island?' Victoria demanded, as though she thought he was keeping something from her. He smiled sweetly.

'Petty details, that's all behind you now, Victoria— the ability to delegate, that's the key.'

She looked suitably irritated. Maltravers crossed his legs. She stared at him.

'It was only my Mundham boatman chap, there's just a chance the old lady might be ill, he thought it could be a good opportunity for us to go trespassing. Still, as you've decided to scrub it—'

'I haven't decided anything. We're here to discuss things. Tell me, Julian, how long do you think it will take for you to stop showing all this petty resentment?'

Maltravers yawned, the most aggressive gesture he felt like making at that moment. The job should have been his. It still could be his, provided he played it cleverly and let her hang herself. It was more or less agreed to shelve Peacock Island.

Later in the cutting rooms Tewson remarked that Victoria had been understandably nervous, taking her first weekly meeting as executive producer.

'I wonder if actual power will mellow our own dear career queen,' said Maltravers.

'You seem to have some compulsion to knock her,' said Tewson, who was always annoyingly calm about other people's problems. 'Don't you like women bosses in principle?'

'I'll let you know when we've seen how it works in practice.'

'Deep down you sure you don't lust after her? Very attractive woman, our Victoria.'

'You think so? I suppose she is, really.' He smiled his sweetly vicious smile. 'Trouble is, old boy, if one did fancy her it would be very one-sided. I don't think sex turns her on. If she ever takes a mate he'll have to be a hero-worshipper.'

Tewson thought about that for a moment.

'And you always used to say she was the bitchy one, Julian.'

The feathered creature was back among the dark rhododendron bushes at the top of the grassy slope. Somewhere near a pair of blackbirds chimed distress notes above a fledgling fallen from the nest into a tangle of dog-roses. A red squirrel froze on the silvery moss that covered the trunk of a misshapen cherry tree. Woodpigeons strutted like fat old squires in plus fours. Then there was the flashing streak of blue down the overgrown lawn.

The tough-skinned feet moved through the dilapidated kitchens, across the vaulted hall and up the great stairway. The rats were already scattering for their holes as the feathered shape moved through the bedroom door.

The deep-set eyes stared across the bed. The familiar

head on the pillow was now an eyeless, fleshless skull fringed by silver hair. Throughout the great spaces of the castle there was absolutely no sound.

You are the curse I have to live with came her voice from the past. Fearful images flashed through the feathered head.

Boom, boom, boom.

The feathered creature was instantly motionless.

Boom, boom.

Somebody was banging the great knocker on the front door of the castle, a sound that had not been heard for more than a decade.

A heavy door screeched on stone.

'Lady Bennett?' came the man's deep voice. 'Lady Bennett? Are you there? It's Greeno, ma'am.'

Silence.

'Lady Bennett? Greeno the boatman, ma'am.'

Heavy footsteps moved across the hall and then began to climb the great stairway. The feathered creature moved soundlessly into the shadows.

CHAPTER THREE

It was twenty to four when Jack Greeno steered the *Mundham Queen* alongside the island jetty, a large and solid structure built by a nineteenth-century owner when the island's clayworks were still paying large profits. Turle climbed up onto the gunwale and used jutting iron hoops to pull himself up onto the black timbers that formed the end of the quay.

'Don't keep us hangin' about,' were Jack's parting words. He was already picking up the megaphone to start the commentary as he stood back to let the boy take the wheel.

Jack resented Lady Bennett, Turle thought as he started up the quay towards the semi-circle of stone cottages. A lot of the town people were the same. Himself, he was as keen on making money as the next man but he still admired the old lady for the way she had always refused to sell or commercialise the island.

Of course, she didn't need the money. Sir Godfrey had left her close on a million pounds—and a pound was still worth twenty shillings in those days—but most women of her age would have sold out long ago and gone abroad, instead of living all alone in a cold castle, cooking for herself on a paraffin stove, eating out of tins, buying more food for the birds than for herself.

Perhaps she was eccentric—clean off her rocker most people said—but what were all the sensible people doing? Turning the countryside into one big car-park, blasting motorways through the forests, polluting the rivers, poisoning the birds and the butterflies. There weren't going to be many places like Peacock Island left soon.

He was a shortish man, Turle Greeno, not especially broad-shouldered but solid, forty-seven years old, a Mundham fisherman all his life, except for five wartime years when he'd served on coastal patrol. A faint smile formed on his weathered face as his turned-down Wellington boots squeaked on the granite that formed the main part of the quay. He was thinking of how Jack would be doing the commentary, just the bare facts, no jokes, and if anybody asked about the legend of the curse he'd sneer and say, 'Old wives' tales, lot of cobblers'.

The air was still and warm among the cottages. Moss and crab grass had almost covered the stone paths. He came into the courtyard in front of the castle.

He walked round, looking up at the leaded windows,

but there was no sign of movement. He tried the door at the rear, frowning when he found it bolted. She always kept that door open. He knocked twice, with no response. He went round again to the front.

Boom, boom, boom. He let the big, black knocker fall three times against the oak door, standing back deferentially, unable to rid himself of the memory of days when a mere boatman would never have dared approach the castle's front door.

Boom, boom. The noise seemed to travel far into the castle's recesses and then return, muffled and unheard by any other ears but his own. He looked at his watch. Still nothing moved inside the castle.

He turned the heavy iron ring. It was very stiff. The door would not open under the pressure of his hand. He put a rubber-booted foot against the bottom edge and leaned his shoulder against the metal-studded oak.

He had to hit the door twice with his whole weight before it shuddered and moved, the bottom edge scraping on stone. He forced it back inch by inch until there was enough space for him to ease through sideways.

For moments his eyes could see very little in the gloom of the great hall.

'Lady Bennett?' he called, not exactly nervous but hesitant. It was the first time he had ever been inside the castle. In the vaulted hall with its dark brown panelling, massive pieces of furniture hidden under dust-sheets, he felt that he had stepped out of the sunlight into some ghostly, secret refuge immune from time.

'Lady Bennett? Are you there? It's Greeno, ma'am.'

His eyes grew accustomed to the light. He tried various doors, all of them locked.

'Lady Bennett?' he called again. 'Greeno the boatman, ma'am.'

Behind the great stairs, to the right, an open passageway took him through low-ceilinged corridors to the kitchens, the original part of the castle. Grey dust covered long black ranges, green mould was thick on sloping draining-boards, dead flies and moths littered the cracked bottom of a long-dry sink.

He went back into the hall. As he started to climb the stairway, with its massive banister and wide, stone steps, he saw paintings—or at least he saw gilt frames surrounding dark rectangles in which could be barely distinguished the vague features of forgotten dignitaries.

He stopped on the landing, looking down over the hall. Such light as came from small windows above the front door was pale and diffuse. The castle was silent.

A faint light came from the far end of a low, dark corridor.

Before he reached the door that hung off one hinge his nostrils received the full impact of the smell. He knew what it was even before he saw what was in the large bed under the canopy.

Other men, realising what they were seeing and smelling, would have panicked, turned their heads, perhaps even fainted. Turle Greeno had been a seaman since the age of fourteen, a member of the lifeboat crew for twenty-five years. Many was the bloated, unrecognisable corpse he had helped drag out of the sea, shrimps hanging from every orifice.

In this dark, stench-ridden chamber, looking down on the white bones of the stripped skull, the only words he muttered were:

'Bloody rats!'

He thought for a moment. He could go back on the boat and notify the police. But that would leave her here with the rats for another hour at least. The island must be crawling with them. He looked round for a chest or wardrobe into which he could put her body. He lifted the corner of a dust-sheet.

Under it were piled four large wooden crates, one of

them carrying a railway label, *Lady Bennett, The Castle, Peacock Island, Mundham Harbour*.

He peered into shadowy corners. To get better light he walked over to the window and took a firm grip on the faded curtains. The rotten fabric crumbled in his fingers. He sneezed as fine dust trickled onto his face. Feathery fragments wafted gently to the floor. Feeling suffocated he tried the window but apparently the leaded frame was not designed to open.

Quickly he made his decision. It would take him only five minutes to meet the boat and tell Jack to inform the police. He would then stay here and keep the rats off until they arrived. He didn't like to think of Lady Bennett alone here at their mercy. He covered her with the heavy brocade bedcover.

Behind the dim outline of a draped wardrobe the feathered creature had watched and listened. When Turle Greeno left the bedroom it waited a second or two and then followed, its hard-skinned feet making only slight scuffing noises on the floor of the dark corridor.

Down the stairs the bare feet slapped on stone. Turle Greeno walked steadily through the gap in the low wall in front of the castle where once there had been ornamental gates.

He headed for the right-angled gap between the grey walls of the third and fourth cottages.

The slapping sound of bare feet reached his ears a second before the awful scream.

Turle Greeno half turned, eyes wide with surprise, stumbling in his thick boots.

Towards him was rushing a squat, feathered shape, a blur of dazzling blue, strange wings beating up into his face, an immensely strong body knocking him backwards, falling, arms flailing, a searing pain in his eyes...

*   *   *

It took half a dozen phone calls to locate Puggy Elder the cameraman. He sounded surprised to hear her voice.

'I tried to ring you,' he said. 'Didn't you get any of my messages?'

'Yes, I did, Puggy,' said Victoria Dryden-Chambers, 'I just wasn't up to ringing you back. I had rather an eventful week, actually. I've been made executive producer here.'

'What—*you* got the job? Congratulations! That's wonderful, Victoria, when can I buy you a drink to celebrate?'

'How about tonight? Better still, why don't we let Artel buy us both dinner? You free?'

'Ehm—tonight? Ehm—yes, oh yes, of course!'

'I'll meet you in the Intrepid Fox—about half past six?'

'Look forward to it, Victoria.'

'So who's the lucky guy?' said Julian Maltravers, standing in the half-open door of her office.

'I'm taking Puggy Elder out to dinner,' she said curtly. 'If it's any of your business.'

'Ah, Victoria,' he said, one hand on his chest, 'I would never dare open my heart to you.'

'Well, if you've no proposition to make and you've finished eavesdropping why don't you just piss off?'

To her disappointment he went without saying anything.

'Isn't he there, then?' Jack Greeno asked as the *Mundham Queen* came round the tip of the island.

'I don't see him,' said the boy.

'We'll go close in and give him a shout.'

Passengers looked on passively as Jack and the boy shouted up the quay. There was no reply.

'Shouldn't I go up and see what's the matter?' asked the boy.

By way of answer Jack opened the throttle and set the boat out towards the channel.

'He's probably havin' a cup of tea with the old bitch,' he growled.

It was half an hour later when the boy vaulted onto the quay and ran towards the cottages, his shaggy blond hair rising and falling about his neck. Jack lit a cigarette.

'I didn't think anybody was allowed on the island,' said a man in white shorts and ankle socks, a camera hanging just above his bulging stomach.

'We're the only ones, we deliver her groceries,' said Jack.

'I hear she keeps savage dogs.'

Jack didn't answer. The boy was coming out from the cottages, walking very slowly.

'Hurry up,' Jack shouted. 'Where's Turle?'

Those who were standing in the boat, heads just above the level of the quay, saw the boy suddenly collapse against the wall of a cottage, his head lolling, his legs partially folding under him.

Cursing loudly, Jack switched off the engine and told the passengers to stay exactly where they were. He climbed onto the quay and walked angrily towards the boy.

'What is it?' he demanded, shaking the boy's shoulders.

'It's Uncle Turle,' the boy said, starting to point and then bursting into tears.

Jack ran between the cottages.

On the moss-covered flagstones of the castle forecourt his brother Turle lay spread-eagled on his back, one knee drawn up, both arms thrown wide.

Where Turle's eyes had been there were now only bloody sockets. His throat had been gashed time and time again. A dark coating of congealing blood lay over

26

the moss and stones on either side of his neck. Blue-bottles and flies swarmed over the torn flesh.

CHAPTER FOUR

'And this is exactly how he was lying when you first saw him?' asked Detective Inspector Victor Daniels of Mundham CID.

'Yes,' said the boy weakly. Jack Greeno nodded in agreement.

'Go back to the boat, sonny,' Daniels said. 'Ingleton, see he's all right.'

The uniformed constable put his arm round the boy's shoulders and they walked off through the gap in the cottages, leaving Jack Greeno, Daniels and Sergeant Bob Gould standing over the corpse. The local doctor who acted as part-time police surgeon, Doctor Barham, was kneeling beside his black medical case.

It was just after five-thirty. Standing as it did at the eastern end of the island the castle was now shaded by the bulk of the island and its tall trees, although out in the harbour the sun was still high and water-skiers and power-boats cut white trails in and out of the moorings.

'He got off the boat about twenty to four?' said Daniels, a youngish, neatly dressed man with a tanned face and severely-parted brown hair.

'Yeah,' said Jack Greeno.

'He came onto the island to see if anything was wrong with Lady Bennett? Why did he think there might be?'

'Her bag of groceries and stuff was still there under the seat on the quay.'

'How did he know the bag hadn't been emptied? She

could have left it there for him to pick up to fetch more stuff.'

'No. He always left the full bag under the seat and when she needed anythin' else she put the empty bag on top of the seat, so's he could see it as we were passin' on the boat.'

'I get it.' Daniels hesitated. 'Sergeant Gould, have a look round inside the castle—might be signs of breaking-in.'

'Very good,' said Gould, an extremely big man with a large belly and fleshy arms. Daniels turned to Greeno. 'You might as well wait in the boat, Mister Greeno.'

'It's okay,' said Jack, his face blank. He started to say something, then changed his mind. He had been going to ask if it were all right for him to do another trip while trade was still at its height. Turle was dead but the rest of them had to go on making a living. Most of the local coppers would have understood but Daniels was a peculiar sort, an outsider. Nobody knew what to make of him.

Daniels dropped to a crouch and opened the small knife he used for cleaning his pipe-bowl. The blade cut into moss and scraped on stone as he marked the outline of the corpse. With his free hand he swatted flies away from his face.

'Let's turn him over now,' he said. The three of them lifted Turle Greeno and laid him down a few feet away, face resting on cool moss. Daniels and Jack Greeno watched as the doctor's fingers probed along the hairline. Then he pulled the shirt-tail out of the trouser belt and bared the dead man's back.

'Mister Greeno, you go back to the boat and wait,' said Daniels.

'I'm okay.'

'I'd rather you did,' Daniels said firmly. Jack Greeno took one last look at his brother's body and turned away. The doctor waited until he was out of sight behind the cottages.

'The only thing I can find is this lump on the back of his head,' he said. 'Judging by its size he must have gone down with a bang.'

'Enough to knock him out?'

'Daze him, maybe.'

'Any idea what was used on his throat?'

The doctor looked uncertain. Contorting his lips he rubbed his small moustache against his nostrils.

'It wasn't a knife or a razor. Look at the scratches on either side.'

They heard Gould's voice. The sergeant's hands could be seen dragging the castle door open a few more screeching inches.

'Well, what would make wounds like that?' Daniels asked. The doctor shook his head slowly.

'Something with a point—look how the skin's been punctured—and then something wider dragged through the flesh.' He stood up. 'I'm giving no firm opinion until I've done the post-mortem—'

'I won't quote you, just give me a rough idea.'

'Well, I've seen that kind of scratching on people who go in for falconry.'

'Falconry?'

They stared at each other. The doctor grimaced. Gould came out onto the front steps of the castle.

'I'm not saying that's what it is.' Barham's voice was defensive and slightly irritable. He was another who never quite knew how to deal with Daniels.

'Oh well, let's see what the post-mortem turns up,' said Daniels. He turned. 'What is it, Sergeant?'

They met a few yards from the low wall that ran round the front of the castle.

'I think you should come upstairs, sir,' said the big,

29

shirt-sleeved man, his helmet towering far above Daniels' head.

Daniels looked back at the doctor.

'Let me know if you see anything else, won't you?'

'Of course I'll let you know,' Barham muttered, pulling a white cloth over the dead man's head as some protection against the flies. The other two went into the castle. Barham drew in a sharp breath. A few yards away a butterfly flitted jerkily above a patch of daisies. A small Tortoiseshell! You didn't see many of them on the mainland nowadays, thanks to all their damned pesticides.

Looking round carefully to make sure nobody was watching, he began to chase it with cupped hands.

Daniels climbed the great stairway a step or two behind the massive buttocks of Sergeant Gould.

'Bit of an old dump, eh?' said Gould.

'No sign of Lady Bennett?'

'The bed's been used—there's a most awful stink. Just through here, better watch your suit, these walls are thick with dust.'

'Doesn't she have any lighting in the place?'

'I tried all the switches, there isn't any power, there was a generator here I think.'

They came into the bedroom.

'You were right about the smell,' said Daniels. He grimaced. 'Rats?'

'Maybe something else as well—see where those curtains have been torn?' The big man looked down at the disordered bed. 'But where might Lady Bennett be, I wonder.'

'It's a biggish island. Did she have a boat?'

'I don't think so. Turle was her only contact with the mainland—I don't think she ever had another boat after the builders were drowned. Were you here then?'

'No. I remember reading about it.'

'You would've been more interested in all those big-time London crimes then, I dare say.'

Daniels showed no reaction to the irony in the sergeant's voice. He was well used to these unsubtle attempts to find out why he had abandoned a brilliant —by Mundham standards anything in London was brilliant—career in the Metropolitan force. As Constable Ingleton came into the bedroom, Daniels was saying:

'We can't do much in this light—no point in us trampling around like a herd of elephants in the dark.'

Gould looked at him sharply, rightly taking the remark as a dig at himself.

'Here's my torch, sir, if you want,' said Ingleton.

The beam moved across fusty drapes.

'What's that beside the bed?' said Daniels, moving round the towering figure of Sergeant Gould. The top of a bedside table was littered with tins of varying sizes, some open, some stacked in shaky piles. Daniels stood over the table, shining the torch into the open tins. He saw touches of green mould on what was left of a canned stew. He moved the light down to the floor.

'It's rats all right,' he said. The beam moved nearer the bed. White porcelain glinted dully. He bent down, lifting the overhanging sheet. 'Good God,' he said, softly.

'What is it?' Gould asked, peering over the Inspector's shoulders.

'It's a very full chamber-pot,' Daniels said emphatically, bumping against the sergeant as he stood up. 'Looks as if she practically lives in this bed. I heard she was eccentric but ... do you know if she has any family?'

'Never heard of any,' said Gould, 'not close relations like.'

'If she has they'll soon turn up,' said Ingleton, 'she's supposed to be worth a million, not counting what the island will sell for.'

'Let's presume she's alive and well until proved otherwise,' said Daniels dryly. 'What's under these dust sheets?'

'Far as I can see, crates of stuff from the Bennetts' other establishment in Somerset,' said Gould. 'They sold that years ago—but these crates have never been opened by the look of 'em.'

'We won't touch anything until it's been gone over for prints,' said Daniels. They left the bedroom. Daniels swung the torch beam across the landing and out over the hall.

'Must've been an impressive sight in the old days,' said Gould.

'Was the front door open?' Daniels asked.

'A bit, hardly enough for me to get through.'

When they descended Daniels told Gould to shut the door from the inside. The sergeant put his seventeen stones against heavy oak. The bottom edge screeched on stone. Daniels saw that one of the hinges was loose. The scratching on the stone was fairly recent.

'What other doors are there?' he asked.

'There's a rear door into the kitchens, sir,' said Gould, 'it was open when I came round. There's a side door facing the church but it looks permanently bolted, there's moss all round the bottom.'

They walked round the outside of the castle. Where once there had been ornamental gardens were now coverts of bramble thorns, nettles, docks and thistles. The remains of low brick walls and some rusted iron-work were all that had survived of an orangery. The decapitated statue of a Roman emperor was a faint gleam of white marble in a heavy cascade of creepers. The iron-studded door of the church of St Aldhelm, built in 1857 on the site of the ancient hermit's chapel, was locked.

The three policemen walked abreast round the wide slope of overgrown lawn that led up from the rear of the castle. This part of the building had low, irregular walls and crooked windows. This was the original 16th-century core to which a succession of rich owners had added crenellated battlements and other castellated monstrosities of the Victorian era.

As they passed between twisted fruit trees small birds chattered in the bushes. A flash of white was the scut of a rabbit bolting from the thick grass round the base of a dead pear tree suffocated by fungus. Higher up the slope, beyond the edge of the clearing, stood the white, leafless skeleton of a tall larch struck many times by lightning.

Soon they were slapping their faces and arms as midges danced above their heads.

From the dark shelter of a giant rhododendron bush a pair of eyes watched the three policemen, the same deep-set eyes that had watched Turle Greeno from the shadows of the bedroom.

Daniels looked at his watch. Thin traces of cloud were turning pink in the early evening sky.

'We'll search the island in the morning,' he said. 'It would be pitch dark before we got men out here tonight —but I want to go over the house as soon as possible —we'll need to rig up lighting—we can be back with the equipment by about half past seven, maybe eight. Meanwhile—somebody's going to have to stay here.'

The young constable kept a very straight face. Gould let out a short laugh.

'I don't think Ingleton's volunteering, praps we'd both better wait.'

'That's okay by me. Ingleton, you fetch the sack from the boat.'

'What sack was that, sir?'

'The canvas sack for the cadaver, of course. And the stretcher.'

The embarrassed constable walked between the cottages. Daniels turned to Gould. What he was going to say would sound fussy, Gould might even take it as a reflection on his intelligence. However, it had to be said.

'Whoever did this is a dangerous madman, Bob,' Daniels said as casually as possible. 'All I want you to do is watch the castle—chase off sightseers—keep an eye out for—'

'Don't fear,' Gould laughed, 'I'll keep both eyes out.'

Daniels turned away to hide his irritation. The Mundham force was rich in eccentric individualism. Gould was just a bigger example, a stout local character full of what could only be described as peasant cunning. He annoyed Daniels intensely. But, he thought, who am I to sneer?

Starting at the feet they pulled the long sack up the stiff, heavy body of the dead boatman and tied the knot above the head. They carried him down the quay on the stretcher.

'We'll have our own launch next time, it'll be a lot quicker,' said Daniels as they slid the stretcher down into the well of the *Mundham Queen*.

As they pulled out into the main channel a brown-skinned man in red bathing-trunks skimmed on water-skis across the big boat's wake. A hundred yards or so away people in yachting clothes were drinking on the decks of elegant cruisers.

'We'll just take a stroll round, eh?' said Gould.

'Nobody would try to land here, anyway,' said Ingleton.

'The Bornless Keeper don't need no boat, lad,' the big man chortled. 'He's here already, no doubt planning some dastardly fate for both of us.'

'You believe in that hoary old crap about a curse, do

you?' said Ingleton with the superior tone befitting one of the new, educated policemen. Gould was noted throughout the force for a reluctance to do paperwork, stemming, it was said maliciously, from an inability to spell.

'Maybe it is old nonsense—still it's a bit of a change from illegal parking—and drunken Dutch seamen,' Gould said cheerfully, making the young constable blush. Ingleton's chief claim to fame was the night he went down to the town quay to arrest three deckhands off a Dutch coaster. They had thrown his helmet into the harbour and then insisted on diving in after it.

'Where do you think Lady Bennett's got to?' he asked, trying to sound unruffled.

'Oh, probably mouldering in some foul crypt or other. You take a look at the cottages, I'll have a walk round the castle—keep a watch on the quay in case we have any callers.'

'If I see the spook I'll scream twice.'

Ingleton smirked as he looked after the sergeant's great back and even larger backside. Gould belonged to bygone days when all a bobby needed were reliable feet and a big fist. Inspector Daniels now, he was more like an up-to-date policeman; that was probably why Gould and the like made fun of him.

Sergeant Gould's size thirteens flattened a trail of crushed grass as he strode round the castle, smiling to himself at some private joke, seventeen stones of terrifying jollity, a great pillar of a man who had never known a moment of fear. He took his helmet off, a massive hand wiping sweat from his brow and then pushing back through a bristly crop of grey hair. There had been a lot of activity, hot work for a man of his weight. He hoped they would be back in the town in time for a few pints before the pubs closed. Or if not, after they had closed.

It was a good many years since he had been on Peacock Island, nineteen-fifty-eight to be precise, when the three builders were drowned. He noticed the changes. Stones had slipped and weeds had grown. Ferns grew high on the wall of the church where a drainpipe ran down from a gutter.

If Lady Bennett was dead the next owner would have to spend a penny or two getting the island right again. And there weren't many private people left with that kind of money. There would be heavy death duties. Whoever inherited it would want to make it a paying proposition. Big tourist attraction, a place like this. The visitors would come in thousands, transistors and beer cans, tea-rooms and ice-cream wrappings, another old chapter closed and forgotten.

He was only forty-five yet in his time he had seen Mundham change, fishing-boats giving way to weekend yachts, seamen's pubs turning into discothèques, old harbour cottages being demolished for high-rise blocks. He could remember his Uncle Ned telling him about Peacock Island, round the coal fire in their little house up by the gasworks, where the fishermen's nets were spread all over the walls and the narrow streets. No cars in those days. A small boy sat with wide eyes as old Ned recited the legend:

Tread ye on this sacred dell the Bornless Keeper ye shall see, pointing the road to Hell.

Aye, old Uncle Ned knew how to spin a yarn. Old wives' tales, of course. The Bornless Keeper, just a yarn to scare little boys and young constables ... but Turle Greeno's body had been real enough. As he stood by the top corner of the old graveyard the big man kept his eyes flicking from shadow to shadow. Of course he was pretty sure the murderer would be well clear by now. Must have had a boat. But what about Lady Bennett? Oh well, she'd probably been scared, old woman gone eccentric in her dotage, she'd have run off and hidden somewhere. Chances were she'd turn up when she saw their lights at the castle.

He hoped so, for he was a kindly man and often when walking along the quays at night he'd look out to Peacock Island and wonder how the old dear was faring on her own, across that dark water.

As he turned to back down the slope a shape darted out of the bushes and stood quite still, apparently watching him.

Gould stopped. He blinked. It had bare legs, he could see that, but the light was bad. Suddenly it darted back into the shrubbery.

He heard it crashing about in the bushes. He ran round behind another bush, hoping to cut off its escape into the woods. He saw it dashing behind a tree. He sprinted forward, letting his helmet fall to the ground.

It was only a few yards ahead, twisting behind a high laurel hedge. Gould turned back and found the end of the hedge. There it was, running across a slight dip, it wasn't running fast, he could catch it easily enough.

When he reached the ruin of an old gazebo it was already at the top of a short slope, head twisting back to look at him. Then it ran out of sight.

Gould reached the top of the slope. He could hear it moving through the woods, twigs crackling, branches swishing. He held one arm up to protect his face.

They were running along a path beside a roofless outhouse. He seemed to be gaining on it. Then it darted ahead.

At last he had it well in sight. It had made a mistake, whatever it was. Gould was at the top of a mossy bank and the shape was only ten yards or so below him, its head turning desperately as it tried to decide which way to run. Ahead of it was a wide belt of knee-high brambles. Gould came pounding down the bank to grab it.

The feathered creature ran straight into the thorny patch. Gould followed without hesitation, big police shoes crashing down on thick stems. Thorns tore at blue serge.

Only five or six yards ahead the creature seemed to be struggling, caught by the creepers.

Even as his great hands and arms lifted to make a running tackle Gould felt his feet coming down on *nothing*. Thorns ripped at his cheeks and eyes as his seventeen stones crashed through a treacherous carpet.

He yelled in terror—for the first time in his life...

CHAPTER FIVE

All through dinner in the Gay Hussar the thick-set, partially bald man in the check shirt and denim suit had hardly taken his eyes off Victoria Dryden-Chambers. She found it hard to conceal her embarrassment. It was not until coffee was poured that she was able to steer the conversation in the intended direction.

'Leaving Artel was the best thing that could have happened to you, Puggy,' she said, allowing him to light her cigarette with her own book of matches.

'Oh yeah,' said Puggy unenthusiastically. 'But I miss the old gang, you know.'

'Mmmm. I thought you might. Funnily enough—' she blew smoke upwards, giving the middle-aged cameraman an entrancing view of her strong throat, '—I've had to let Darcy go, had you heard? The work-flow isn't consistent enough to justify a staff man's wage.' She looked at him, frowning slightly as if struggling with an emerging idea. 'I wonder—you saying you miss the old gang is giving me an idea—'

'What I mean is—I miss you, Victoria,' he said, almost blurting the words out. 'You know what I ...' He stared at his hands, which were fiddling with her book of matches '... You know how I feel about you, Victoria.'

'You're very sweet, Puggy,' she said quietly, eyes downcast in what might have looked like demure shyness but was in fact repugnance. Not because of Puggy, he was harmless if a bit naïve, no, repugnance at what she was doing. It had been one of the happiest moments of her life when he had left the company and she had thought she would never again have to fend him off. Still, there had to be some compensation for the disadvantages a woman suffered in this racket.

Without changing her tone she went on:

'I've got to make a success of Artel,' she said. 'I mean, to hold onto this job I've got to prove I'm actually better than anyone else ...'

'I'm sure you'll—'

'I need help though. They're not all on my side. Julian, for instance—well, you know what he's like.'

'Jealous as hell, I know. Still—'

'Puggy, would you possibly consider helping me out? No, just a moment till you hear it. I've only just thought of it. Would you possibly consider letting me pay you a retainer for first call on your services?'

This surprised Puggy. In fact, for a moment it hurt him. It wasn't *him* she wanted, it was his skill. His fingers straightened out the mangled matchbook. Since the big upheaval at Artel he had become one of the busiest freelances in the business. Two programmes he had shot had won international awards and his going rate these days was way out of Artel's class. He knew all that. He was also intelligent enough to suspect he was merely suffering from a middle-aged hunger for the romance of youth.

Knowing all these things, however, did not lessen the anguish. He said he would think about it, making some excuse about his tax position.

When they were on the pavement in Greek Street he offered to drive her home to St John's Wood. She said she could easily get a cab but allowed him to insist. They got into his big Ford estate car, which was parked in Soho Square. She had to wait until he lifted a lot of junk off the passenger seat.

He hardly spoke until he was shutting off the engine outside the modern block of flats near Lord's cricket ground. He had made up his mind. It was no good if she only wanted him behind a camera. He turned towards her.

'Come up for a drink,' she said.

As he followed her into the lift he found himself trembling like an adolescent.

Half an hour later he was back in the car, hands still trembling. Their first kiss! Just a quick peck on the lips—but he knew what it meant. Tonight she had been tired and tense, he had understood without her having to say anything, in fact it was he who had insisted on leaving when her headache started—but he knew now, it was all going to turn out the way he had dreamed.

He started the engine, then rolled down the window to look up at the seventh floor. He saw a light. Perhaps it wasn't her window, it didn't matter.

Humming gaily, he made a snappy U-turn and drove off towards North Ealing and his wife and five children.

First of all nobody knew where to find a portable generator. Then the civilian fingerprint man was not at home and contrary to regulations had not left a number where he could be contacted. His wife thought he might be in any of several pubs. Daniels sent a car to look for him. He allowed himself no irritation. It was not his responsibility whether this force was efficient or not. He asked the switchboard girl to get him the Chief Constable.

Everything was under control. The Coastguard and Harbour-Master's staff were looking out for any strange or suspicious craft. Neighbouring police forces had been alerted. Men were being detailed to form tomorrow's main search party. Mobile patrols were covering as much of the harbour's fifty-mile shoreline as possible.

'We've got the Chief Constable for you now, sir,' said the switchboard girl.

Daniels took the call standing by his desk. He felt very tense. It was the most dramatic crime Mundham had known in years and with Alf Groves on holiday he was in sole charge. Most men would have been jumping for joy at being in his position.

It didn't take the Chief Constable long to ask the inevitable question:

'Well, Inspector, do we call Superintendent Groves back from Wales?'

'It's your decision, of course, sir,' said Daniels.

'I know what Alf would want.'

'Yes, sir.'

'And what would you like me to do?'

'I don't have any opinion on it, sir.'

'That surprises me, Daniels. Most officers would be only too glad to have a case like this chucked in their laps. You don't doubt your own capabilities, do you?'

'No, sir.'

'You wouldn't be worrying about what Groves will say, would you?'

'No, sir.'

'I should hope not. Anyway, I do not propose to make panic calls to Superintendent Groves. When he returns

I shall let him know it was my decision.'

'You want me to carry on with it then, sir?'

'I do. I'll be here at home if you want me.'

'Very good, sir. If we come up with anything tonight I'll be in touch immediately.'

For a moment he thought of ringing Groves at his hotel in Wales. Alf wouldn't wait to be asked officially, a case like this would have him dashing back overnight. He picked up the phone again. When the switchboard girl asked what number he wanted he chewed his lower lip. How could he explain it to anyone else?

'Get me my wife, please,' he said. She did not sound too disappointed when he said he would not be home that night. In fact, when he told her about the murder she became enthusiastic.

'It's time you showed them what you can do,' she said.

'Why?'

'Oh come on, Victor, you can't kid me, you know very well you shouldn't be taking orders from a dunderhead like Alf Groves. All this business about a quiet life—it's not good for you—'

'Nonsense, I'm thriving on it.'

'I don't mean the quiet life, I mean deliberately forcing yourself to work below your capabilities. It wasn't my idea to leave London, I hope you remember that.'

'I don't regret a thing. I'll ring you in the morning.'

On the return journey across the three miles of harbour to the island Daniels stood in the stern of the crowded launch. Behind them the town's waterfront pubs and cafés and souvenir shops and shellfish stalls merged into a single blaze of light. Farther round the harbour he could see lines of red lights on the road from the Monks Sweep car-ferry, holidaymakers' cars returning from a long day on the heathland beaches. The air was soft and warm on his cheeks. Through a fuzz of static from the launch radio he could hear the little waves slapping against the hull.

It was exactly for moments like this that he had come to Mundham. Capabilities, funny that both the Chief and Lisa should use the same word; couldn't they understand that a man might dislike the job he was skilled at? That he might positively enjoy the dullness of Mundham, the comfortable routine of small burglaries, petty embezzlement by shop assistants, the occasional case of child cruelty? Mundham was so backward it didn't even have a drug problem and that made him like it all the more.

It was almost dark as the powerful spotlight picked out the castle quay. He saw Ingleton's solitary figure standing at the edge, hand shielding his eyes. The launch bumped against massive timbers. Ingleton stood above them, peering down, face agitated.

'Seen the ghost, then?' somebody called from the boat.

Daniels climbed up the iron rungs.

'It's Sergeant Gould, sir,' Ingleton said anxiously, 'I can't find him!'

'Playing hide-and-seek, were you?' Daniels said. 'Come on, you chaps, get that stuff unloaded, we don't want—'

'I'm not joking, sir,' Ingleton said. 'I haven't seen him for more than an hour. I was checking the cottages, he went round the castle, he never came back. I've been all round here looking for him.'

'Stupid big—' Daniels took in a sharp breath. 'Begg, soon as you've got everything off take the launch round the island, use the loud-hailer, lights, everything, I want Gould back here on the double. Use the radio if you see anything.'

It took about twenty minutes to get the generator set up and cables led into the castle. The unshielded arc lights gave the sombre bedroom the brilliance of a stage set, the faces of the policemen unnaturally pale and their chins exaggeratedly dark. Daniels watched them start to work. The kneeling fingerprint man was stroking a bedpost with a brush.

When the launch returned he went down the quay to use its radio.

'No sign of Sergeant Gould, sir,' said Constable Begg.

'He's big enough to take care of himself,' Daniels said calmly. When the big man turned up he would give him a roasting. Not that it bothered him that Gould never called him 'sir', but disobeying orders was going too far. Sometimes you had to throw your weight about, just to make people aware that you weren't soft. The quiet life had to be fought for, just like any other.

He had finished speaking to Inspector Titmus, who was getting the search party and the dog teams arranged, when the radio room policewoman told him that Sergeant Butler wanted to speak to him. As he waited Daniels changed his weight to the other foot, making the launch roll slightly in the water. Butler was a highly ambitious young man, he thought, he would give his right arm to be in charge of this case.

'Just to let you know, sir, that Superintendent Groves phoned in about twenty minutes ago. He said to inform you that he'll be with you in the morning.'

'Just happened to phone in, did he?'

'Yes, sir, he phoned from Wales, he said he was just calling out of boredom, seemingly there's a drought in Wales and he can't do any fishing.'

'That was lucky, then,' Daniels said.

'I thought you'd want to know, sir.'

I'll bet you did, Daniels thought. I bet you just loved the idea of telling me that my brief moment of glory was over. Given half a chance he was sure he could easily come to dislike Butler intensely.

As he walked back up the quay, seeing policemen's silhouettes moving against bright lights in the small upstairs windows of the castle, he told himself that luck was on his side. He had a strong feeling this might not be a simple case. It would be interesting to watch Alf Groves blundering through it.

As she prepared for bed Victoria Dryden-Chambers switched on the colour TV. Having changed into severely practical cotton pyjamas and an ankle-length dressing-gown, she warmed some milk and placed the mug and the bottle of sleeping-tablets on the coffee-table.

As she flopped back into the black leather sofa she sighed, partially with relief at having got rid of Puggy so easily, partly from the sheer exhaustion of the evening; trying to be bright yet impersonal, ignoring Puggy's clammy stare, enduring his heavy grip on her arm, choosing each word carefully so as not to give him any illusions, then having to act out the charade of the headache...

The phone rang.

It was Julian.

For a moment she could hardly speak. It wouldn't take a moment to get dressed again.

But Julian had not phoned to suggest that he might drop round for a drink.

'I thought you might like to know there's been a new development on that island project you scrubbed this afternoon,' he said, so casually, so maliciously. 'My boatman chap's just rung—pity we didn't go ahead with it earlier, we'd be sitting on some valuable exclusive footage...'

'Save me the build-up, Julian,' she snapped.

'Arouse you from the virginal bed, did I? Sorry about that. Anyway, it seems that the phantom has struck

45

again, very bizarre...'

He told her about the savage murder of the boatman. As she listened she felt her tiredness evaporate.

'...goes to show, doesn't it?' he concluded. 'Without Darcy standing by we've no chance of covering it.'

'No?' She could well imagine the patronising smile on his face. She made up her mind very quickly. Now was as good a time as any to put Julian straight. 'We can be down there tomorrow night,' she said. 'You fix the boatman, we'll take Jock Weir, I'll—'

'I thought we'd scrubbed Peacock Island, darling.'

'It was only a boring travelogue then. What was it you said, we had to be quick and flexible?'

'And imaginative. Where do you imagine we'll find a cameraman this late for a rush weekend job?'

'Oh, didn't I tell you? I've just fixed up with Puggy Elder to work for us on a retainer. He's free this weekend, I'll ring him when he gets home. You'd better ring Jock.'

'Are you drunk, Victoria?'

'No, are you? I think we should take your car, Puggy's smells of sticky children.'

'Listen, my dear, that island will be crawling with policemen, what possible—'

'Send Jock down in advance, then, he can find out exactly what's happening.'

For a moment he was silent. With a conscious effort she stopped herself from breaking the silence. When Julian spoke she could tell he had correctly appraised her mood.

'Yes, it might well be worth a little trip down there. Shouldn't be too difficult for Jock and Puggy and myself to sneak onto the island for an hour or two—'

'I'll be coming, Julian.'

'Oh? Why?'

'It's what good executive producers do, isn't it? It'll

be fascinating for me to watch you being quick and flexible and imaginative. Besides, weekends can be so boring in the virginal bed.'

Being Julian, of course, he had to have the last word. 'Is that part of your deal with Puggy?' he drawled, 'instant togetherness?'

'You bitchy bastard,' she said—after he had rung off.

By midnight they had searched the castle, which Daniels realised was only a normal country house with external pretensions. Apart from the bedroom it showed no sign of recent habitation. They found no trace of the missing Lady Bennett. The only evidence that she ever penetrated any other part of the house apart from the gloomy bedroom on the first floor was in a locked cupboard in the low-ceilinged kitchen.

Forcing it open they found it stacked with unopened tins, some of which fell out onto the stone floor as Daniels examined the labels. Most of the cans were popular brands of dog and cat foods but he also recognised cheap lines of meat stews, pork sausages in baked beans, assorted grills that required only re-heating to be allegedly digestible.

'And she's supposed to be worth millions?' said a disgusted detective constable.

'Jack Greeno said her dog died about three years ago,' Daniels said. 'I wonder if she's been eating pet foods herself.'

'Amazing what queer things they'll do, them old idiots.'

A constable found Daniels to tell him Doctor Barham wanted to speak to him. Walking down the quay Daniels saw the sweeping arc of car headlights on the road to the Monks Sweep ferry. Lights were shining from the portholes of the moored motor-cruisers and across the black, whispering water came faint strains of music.

He climbed down into the launch and took the radio-telephone from Constable Begg.

Barham was able to confirm that the throat wounds had caused Greeno's death, his windpipe having been severed. It was impossible to tell if the eyes had been torn out before or after death.

'Any new thoughts on the type of weapon?' asked Daniels. Even through the fuzzy crackling he could hear Barham hesitating.

'Certainly claw-shaped,' he said. 'I should also tell you that I found one or two animal hairs round the wounds —I've sent them to the County General laboratories for examination but they're almost certainly rabbit hairs.'

'Rabbit hairs?'

'My guess is they were adhering to the murder weapon and were transferred during the attack.'

'Are you sure?' was all Daniels could think of saying.

'I'm not making any more guesses, thank you. By the way, has it occurred to you that we didn't find the eyes? I had a look for them when you were in the castle ... goodnight.'

Daniels went back to the castle and climbed the stairway to the first-floor landing. As he looked down over the hall he told himself there had to be a straight-forward explanation. The strange contours of furniture under dust-sheets began to look like sleeping ghosts. He looked at his watch. Gould had been missing now for five hours.

He found himself shivering slightly. Only the night chill, of course. He went through the low corridor to the bedroom. There *had* to be a simple explanation for everything, Greeno's savage mutilation, the disappearance of Lady Bennett, Gould's disappearance.

'*Claws?*' he murmured to himself, frowning. What would Alf Groves make of that?'

CHAPTER SIX

By eight o'clock thirty uniformed constables and two dog teams were assembled in front of the castle. Detective Superintendent Alf Groves and the unshaven Daniels, who had been on the island all night, were examining a map. The Alsatian dogs sat quietly on the ends of slack leashes.

'Well, it's only eighty years out of date,' Groves said, flicking the photostatted map with his middle finger.

'We were lucky to get it,' Daniels said quietly.

Somebody at the Central Police Station had remembered seeing an old map of the island in the town library and a Panda car was sent to the home of the borough's chief librarian at three in the morning. He was taken through the deserted town to the library building. From the closed shelves of the archives section he produced a slim history of the island privately published for one of its Victorian owners. The map was a fold-out and Mr Llewellyn had reacted indignantly when the Panda car driver went to tear it out.

Not that Mr Llewellyn wasn't keen to assist the police. He agreed most readily to take the precious volume to the Central Police Station where the map could be photo-copied. His somewhat surprising enthusiasm was partly due to insomnia and partly to the fact that for the previous eleven years he had been writing a definitive history of Mundham. It was not often a historian could participate personally in his chosen subject.

He was disappointed when the police proved unwilling to let him accompany the search party which left Gallow Quay in the early dawn light, but instead of going home he walked back slowly through the town to the library building.

Although he was in his sixties he was full of bustle as he unlocked the archives section door once again and dragged a massive volume from a bottom shelf. Under an angle-lamp he began to turn yellowing pages of the bound editions of the local paper. As the large sheets crackled between his fingers he hummed his favourite tune, the Czarist national anthem.

Something had struck a faint chord in his memory, something about the way Turle Greeno had been killed ...

Detective Superintendent Groves looked skywards. The sun was barely up but already it was very warm on the island.

'So where is this damned helicopter?' he demanded. Groves, who had driven all night to get back from Wales, invariably scoffed at other people's brainwaves, unless they worked, when he would claim them as his own. When he first heard that Daniels had asked the Navy for a helicopter he'd said, 'I'm surprised you didn't ask for the Marines as well'. Now he regarded the helicopter as essential and seemed to be blaming Daniels for its non-appearance. Daniels showed no resentment.

Groves was a tall man with stooped, narrow shoulders and a sagging belly. He wore a flat cloth cap and a cardigan under a tweed jacket which had leather elbow-patches. Daniels always thought he looked more like a market-gardener than a senior detective.

As usual he had a cigarette in his mouth. He was not a chain-smoker but once he had one lit he kept it between his lips until the soggy end, blowing ash off onto his clothes. People often told him that doctors reckoned this to be the most lethal way of smoking. To which Groves usually replied, 'Them and their damned statistics, everything's bad for you if you believe *them*.'

Groves was not so wilfully ignorant as this typically small-town attitude suggested; Daniels had come to realise that his most stupid remarks were meant satirically. From the Chief Constable down the Mundham police force—indeed, a large part of the town—regarded him as a sport, curmudgeonly and eccentric perhaps, but *shrewd*.

Daniels felt his teeth on edge whenever he was near the man. In the three years he had been at Mundham he had fended Groves off with a front of formal politeness.

This morning Groves was acting true to form. As they waited for the Navy's helicopter he again went over what Daniels had done since Greeno's murder, never putting it into so many words but making it obvious he expected to find mistakes and omissions. Daniels showed no resentment. Nothing that happened in Mundham could ever affect him emotionally. He had put all that behind him. His salary and his pension, that was all this job meant to him now. On the other hand it did give him a certain private amusement to watch Groves' attempt to make his dash from Wales seem vitally important.

They had established that fingerprints in the castle were either Greeno's or those of a smaller hand, presumably that of the missing Lady Bennett. As far as the search was concerned Daniels had made every necessary preparation. Constable Ingleton had confirmed his order to Gould not to leave the castle vicinity. It was not his fault the Mundham constabulary did not include a metal detector in its equipment. Yet all the time Groves sucked on his disgusting cigarette and kept a faint sneer on his face.

Daniels was relieved when they heard the first faint chugging of the helicopter coming across the harbour. A few more minutes and Groves might have succeeded in needling him.

'Right, then, let's get on with it,' Groves said.

Three constables were left to watch the castle and the quay. The others were split into two parties, each fanning out in line behind a dog-team. Constables exhaled the last smoke from stamped-out cigarettes. A whistle blew.

They had barely rounded the castle when the Alsatian with Daniels' section picked up a trail. Pulling firmly on its leash it took the handler up the graveyard wall. Then it hesitated.

'Two tracks here, sir,' was the handler's interpretation of the dog's indecision. 'One through the wall here —the other goes across the grass.'

'Try the graveyard first,' said Daniels.

The line of constables stopped, all eyes on the brown and black dog. It nosed in a straight line across the graveyard until it came to a gravestone, a white marble warrior, helmeted, crossed gauntlets holding the hilt of a sword which rested down chest and stomach.

The dog sniffed round the warrior. Then it started towards the church. A forest of nettles did not deter its nose-down progress to the other side of the graveyard. Daniels came down off the tumbled stones of the broken wall.

'He wants to go into these rhododendron bushes, sir,' the handler called.

'Why was he so interested in this item, then?' Daniels said, prodding the warrior's chain-mail ribs with his toe. The gilt had not quite worn off the carved lettering at the foot: *Sir Godfrey Bennett, M.C., Born 1893 Died 1943.* Daniels noted the absence of terms of endearment. That class believed in the stiff upper lip. He peered around the stone. Lots of rabbit droppings. Then he looked along the line the dog had followed. Someone might have come down from the bushes, crossed the graveyard to the gap in the wall, stopping at the stone for some reason—perhaps using it as a cover?

He gave the word for the line of constables to move forward. Trying to keep the dog-handler in sight Daniels soon realised how difficult the search was going to be. The brambles were the worst, constables often having to make five-yard detours to pass great outcrops of thorny shoots. They would need billhooks if they were to make an inch-by-inch search for the missing murder weapon.

He pressed the transmission switch on the little radio. 'Anything up there, Broomhead?' he said into the black plastic casing.

'Scent's still pretty strong—I'm about twenty yards to your left, sir, slightly higher up—you'll see a patch of bamboo.'

'Bamboo?'

'That's what it looks like.'

The yellowing stalks towered high above their heads, giving Daniels the fanciful but none the less real sensation that he was taking part in a farcical film. He expected a white hunter to appear in a pith helmet.

He could hear the helicopter now but not see it. On the old map this was a path, Bowery Walk, although it was so overgrown it was impossible to see more than twenty yards ahead, sometimes less. The island was a much better place to hide in than he had imagined. It was a lot bigger than it looked from the town quays.

The path ran along the north shore, often no more than a tunnel under the branches of oaks, white poplars, sycamores, cedars, here and there a giant elm. Through gaps in the alders and hawthorns growing on the reedy ground between the path and the water he got occasional glimpses of the shore, a wide expanse of mud and shallow water on which flocks of seabirds searched for sandworms and small fish stranded by the tide, seagulls, wild duck, oyster-catchers, long-legged waders, a small contingent of wild geese. One thing was sure, nobody could escape off the island in that direction. A man would be over his head in slime before his feet touched solid bottom.

Yet when they caught up with Broomhead and the dog it was urgently waiting to follow the trail into the thick scrub that lay between the path and the harbour mud.

'Go very carefully,' said Daniels, 'look out for holes.'

They watched man and dog wade knee-deep into coarse grass. Daniels checked the map. Just about here was marked *Roman bath*.

The dog-handler shouted.

'He wants that hiker's staff, sir,' said a constable.

Daniels took the Boy Scout pole out to Broomhead, gingerly picking his way on yielding ground, hoping that his shoes would not get wet.

'He wants to go straight into that lot,' said Broomhead. In front of them was a wide spread of brambles. About halfway across they could see a gaping hole in the creepers, thin shoots hanging down into darkness. It looked fairly recent.

The dog was tense. Daniels prodded into the mass of creepers. He took a cautious step forward. Again the staff touched solid ground. He moved forward a yard, trying to tramp the thickest bramble shoots safely underfoot.

Then the Boy Scout pole sank down as far as he could reach.

It took them five or six minutes, using boots, batons, lengths of dead branch and nervous hands, to discover that this thorny vegetation covered a sunken area about the size of a small house, with a dividing wall running across the middle.

Originally there had been a wooden platform covering the ruins of the old Roman bath but the planks had long ago rotted, leaving the creepers to form a false ceiling.

Gradually they pulled the mass of shoots clear.

Broomhead stepped onto the top of the dividing wall. Daniels walked round the edge.

'Oh no!' he gasped.

He was looking down at the lifeless body of Sergeant Gould, one shirt-sleeved arm stretched forward on the floor where Roman centurions had bathed.

Flies and bluebottles were buzzing over what had been the big man's head.

CHAPTER SEVEN

The two senior detectives sat on the low wall in front of the castle. It was typical of Groves, Daniels thought, to be munching happily at sandwiches so soon after seeing what had happened to Gould.

Eight men had been required to lift the sergeant's corpse out of the Roman bath. It was now in a polythene sack on a launch heading across the harbour. Groves belched on a bottle of beer.

'I made it clear he wasn't to leave the castle vicinity,' Daniels said, slapping at his cheek. They had discovered that the island was home to many biting insects including, to their surprise, mosquitoes. Vicious mosquitoes at that.

'Independent sort of bugger was Big Bob,' said

Groves, mouth temporarily bereft of cigarette as he chewed noisily on ham and white bread. 'Point is, why did he go off?'

'Must have seen somebody, chased after him, crashed into the bath.'

'Why smash his head in, then?'

'I think we're up against some kind of lunatic.'

'Oh yes? And why is this lunatic on the island in the first place?'

'Stands to reason there ought to be stuff worth stealing in a house like this—paintings, silver, antiques, maybe even a bundle of cash knowing what eccentric old ladies are like...'

Daniels hesitated. He was, as usual, being milked by Groves. It was called team-work. Groves would take all the credit. On the other hand, this was why he had come to Mundham in the first place, wasn't it? The quiet life, without the responsibility?

'Don't keep any secrets,' Groves said, holding his mouth open to give another belch a chance.

'Greeno might have surprised this man—it's highly possible we'll find he's done for Lady Bennett as well. So he attacks Greeno—could be Greeno recognised him. He hasn't time to take whatever it is he's stealing from the house before Jack and the boy discover Greeno's body. So he hangs about in the bushes waiting for a chance to get back into the house. He sees most of us go off in the boat, he sneaks out, Gould sees him, chases him—and runs head first into the bath.'

'He's a trifle on the violent side for a common housebreaker, isn't he?'

'Unless he's a simple lunatic.'

'Or wants us to think he is.' Groves used the nail of an index finger to scrape something caught in his irregular teeth. 'Anyway, we know he's off the island, that trail our dog picked up went straight into the water, just this side of the cliffs, he probably had a boat there, rubber dinghy maybe hidden in the trees. Jack Greeno said they didn't see any boat near the island, didn't he?'

'Why did you say he wanted us to think he's a madman?'

Groves tilted a third bottle of beer to his mouth. He wiped his lips, belched and spat.

'Identification,' he said. 'That's why they were both killed, they recognised him.' He lit a cigarette and flicked the match at a family of sparrows scavenging the crumbs from his sandwiches. 'You're probably right about one thing. My guess is he deliberately showed himself to Gould, to entice him away from the castle. He must have known that bath is a natural trap. Then he was intending to come back to get whatever it was he wanted from the castle. For all we know he did get it.'

'Lady Bennett's the only one who could tell us that.'

'It'll be a miracle if she isn't lying dead somewhere.'

'The dogs should have turned her up.'

'That's another thing tells me we're looking for a local bloke. This island must have plenty of places you could hide a body, if you know them. Anyway, while we've got all these lads we might as well use them. That map shows two old wells for a start. And the house— old place, probably got cellars we don't know about. Better give the church a good going over. Of course he could just have tied a stone round her neck and slung her in the harbour. Anyway, give the place a thorough going-over this afternoon—'

'Aren't you going to be here?'

'Oh no, there's a lot to be done back at the station. I'll get onto the Bennett family solicitors, inform the next-of-kin, see who holds an inventory of the castle contents, maybe it's in a will or something.' He stretched and yawned without removing the cigarette from his lower lip. 'Idyllic spot, isn't it? It's years since I saw so many butterflies. No pesticides, of course.'

For a moment he sounded so pleasant and relaxed Daniels was tempted into responding.

'We saw Barham chasing a wretched butterfly last night when he thought we weren't looking. There he was, running round Greeno's body with his hands grabbing at it!'

'A true enthusiast.'

'One thing he did say . . .'

'Yes?'

'This weapon we're looking for.'

'Oh yes,' said Groves briskly, standing up. 'Claws, eh? Rabbit hairs on the dead man's face? I've often wondered about Barham—'

'He says he's seen that type of wound on people who've been attacked by falcons.'

'Down came a blackbird and pecked out his eyes?' Groves sneered unbelievingly. 'Or maybe a man-eating bunny-rabbit? A billhook, that's my guess. Claws! I hope he shows as much imagination with his National Health patients.'

'So what happens if we get caught on this bloody murder island?' growled Puggy Elder. He was on the back seat of the Peugeot estate car, sprawled between a pile of nylon parkas, holdalls and other gear that wouldn't fit into the open boot with the big camera case and the cans of exposed film.

'Keep the camera rolling till you hit the water, mate,' said Maltravers, who was driving. 'Remember the Falls Road job?'

'We won't have an IRA escort this time.'

In the front passenger seat, one white-trousered leg drawn up under her so she could sit facing the long, indolent figure of Maltravers, Victoria Dryden-

Chambers smiled as she placed a heavily-ringed hand on the shoulder of his corduroy jacket. They heard Puggy drawing in a sharp breath. He drew a folded copy of the *Angling Times* out of his jacket pocket.

Maltravers stretched his neck to get a look at Puggy in the rear-view mirror. His eyes met Victoria's and she winked. Maltravers smiled knowingly, not for the reason Victoria imagined.

The fact that Puggy should be in love with Victoria of all people really was a stupendous joke, Maltravers thought. You only had to look at him, forty-six years old, hardly attractive even by today's ugly-cult standards, married miserably with five children, brilliant behind a camera but naïve and awkward in almost every other respect.

Yet there he was, eating his heart out, just waiting for her to give the signal, a drop of her false eyelashes perhaps, then he'd be instantly prepared to abandon wife, home, children, career, sanity itself.

All for *Victoria*!

That was the funniest part of it. Victoria?

It passed all understanding. Still, it was proving useful. God knows what ecstasies she had dangled before Puggy to coax him into taking a first-call retainer from a shaky outfit like Artel.

You poor love-sick, middle-aged dope, Maltravers thought, hearing Puggy turn the pages of his fishing paper.

Victoria yawned. They had been driving for two hours and she was far too sophisticated to enjoy scenery.

'Did they say on the news whether they've caught this fiend?' she asked, her hand still on Maltravers' shoulder.

'Never mind the murderer, it says in the papers they've stopped anyone going near this bloody island of yours, Julian.'

'What's the worst they can do to us?' said

Maltravers. 'Trespass? Think of it as a challenge and an adventure, mes enfants.'

'Let's hope Jock stayed sober long enough to fix up another boatman,' said Victoria.

Puggy stared at the curve of her arm resting on the back of the seat. For a moment he had a maddening urge to lean forward and kiss her elbow. He did not understand how Julian could just sit there, driving mile after mile with her hand touching him. Unless it was true after all, what some people said about Julian.

His eyes met Maltravers' in the mirror and he quickly looked down at his paper. Maltravers began to hum softly.

Poor Puggy, he thought, if I told him the truth he wouldn't believe me.

The police squads started off on their second search of the island. Out in the harbour, only a few hundred yards away, a squadron of sailing dinghies tacked in unison before a breeze that rippled the water into cascades of golden pinpoints. Stubby cabin-cruisers ploughed energetically towards Monks Sweep. Suntanned people sprawled on the decks of large motor-yachts nosing off to exotic places far from the holiday masses. On the seaward side of Monks Sweep the beaches were a hubbub of splashing children, deck-chairs, canvas wind-breaks, plastic balls, rubber rafts.

But the island air was still and humid. Martins dipped and dived about the church tower. A trio of geese came over the castle in a V-formation, wingbeats audible as they started their descent to the mudflat feeding grounds. From the woods came the rasping screams of peacocks.

The sweating lines of blue-shirted constables flushed several pairs of golden pheasants. The vibrations of their heavy steps broke up the siestas of slow-worms and lizards. They interrupted—almost indecently it might have seemed to the sensitive—the strutting rituals of peacocks, magnificently splayed tails rustling urgently to impress dowdy hens apparently more interested in pecking insects among the grass.

They saw red squirrels, and the more knowledgeable in natural history explained how the imported grey squirrel had driven the native red almost to extinction on the mainland.

They saw spotted coaltits, long-tailed tits, chaffinches, even the tiny gold-crested wren. They started rabbits of many colours, descendants of several pairs of fancy bucks and does brought to the island half a century before to amuse some Edwardian gentleman's children. They saw the tip of a vast underground nest of wood ants. They heard the muffled drilling of woodpeckers.

They passed the blue, lifeless waters of the clay pool and then the stagnant, lily-covered waters of an old ornamental lake over which iridescent dragonflies skimmed and hovered away their one short day in the sun.

They searched the ruins of old cottages and the starker remnants of the pottery works. In a crumbling farm shed, where hay still lay in crude wooden racks, they saw the rusting grandeur of a de Dion Bouton car standing where it had been last parked during the First World War, tyres long since perished, upholstery hidden under a veneer of orange fungus spores.

They lowered men into long-dry wells, into a darkness that had not been broken for a hundred years or more.

On the brass wings of the lectern eagle in front of the church altar they saw a massive, brass-clasped Bible lying open at the second chapter of Deuteronomy, the fading type spotted by rusty blotches.

Finally they searched the deep, cold waters under the

castle quay, but, like all the other searchers, the emerging frogman could only shake his head...

Daniels knelt over the side of the launch, cupping some icy water in his palms and splashing it over his tired, stubbly face. Wearily he climbed up onto the quay. If he didn't get some sleep soon he would pass out on his feet. The word was quickly passed round to get into the launches.

'There's just a chance this maniac will come back,' Daniels said to Sergeant Willey, who was being left in charge of a small party to patrol the castle area. 'Keep in pairs, you've all got your radios, if—'

'We'll be all right, sir,' the sergeant said airily.

'Gould thought he knew it all as well,' Daniels snapped. Climbing back into the launch he regretted losing control of his temper. As they were untying the mooring ropes he shouted up to Sergeant Willey: 'Stay in pairs even when you go for a piss, this force is short enough of men as it is.'

Most of the constables laughed at Willey. Just for a moment Daniels felt the warmth of popularity. He told the launch driver to take the long way back to Mundham, round the southern side of Peacock Island.

The tide was ebbing, fast currents churning towards the eastern tip of the island where they converged with the main tidal flow racing towards the narrow channel of Monks Sweep and the sea. The launch kept about thirty yards off the shore to avoid smooth whirls and eddies whipping over submerged rocks.

Daniels shaded his eyes with his hand as they moved into the late afternoon sun. He saw the low, rocky stretch where the tracker dog had followed a trail down to the water's edge. From here the island was about a mile off the mainland shore, a desolate waste of reedy inlets stretching inland to the vast, treeless heath. Local duck-hunters must be the only people who would know those marshy inlets.

The fawn-coloured cliffs rose suddenly from a narrow belt of low boulders exposed only at low tide. They were about sixty feet high, the top edge obscured by ferns and small trees and bushes seemingly frozen in the act of falling. Over the centuries the tidal current had eaten into the cliffs and here and there they hung out over the water. The dogs had followed a trail that led along the top of the cliffs but from here it was obvious that they were too steep to climb. He told the driver to head for the town.

The launch engine revved up and they cleaved through the oncoming current, turning at the jutting black piles of the old clayworks jetty and heading across the harbour.

As the noise of the launch engine faded the squat, feathered creature pulled itself back into the dark tunnel, its movements accompanied by faint cracklings and scrapings from a carpet of broken eggshells.

They had gone and The Keeper could sleep until it was dark.

The Red Lion at Beckham was a low, white-walled cottage standing opposite the village's surprisingly large stone quay, a relic of days when a constant flow of barges from the Peacock Island pottery works delivered daily loads of bricks, tiles, chimney-pots, drainpipes and other terracotta and glazed clay products that had helped to make an assortment of Victorian speculators richer than they were already.

At one end of the quay lay three barges converted into slummy house-boats. A few yachts' masts stuck up above the edge of the quay. Taking off his dark glasses Maltravers rubbed his eyes and stretched his arms.

'Charming little spot,' said Victoria mockingly. The car was facing the inlet, which opened out into the western end of the vast Mundham harbour.

'Let's find Jock and get a drink,' said Puggy. 'I'm knotted with cramp.'

'What do they gargle in these rustic nookeries?' Victoria drawled as they began to get out of the car. 'Rough cider with a dash of dead rat, drowned but not shaken?'

Maltravers locked the doors.

'Just one thing,' he said, 'we all know how erotic the sweaty masses find a television camera but don't give them the slightest hint that we're going onto the island.'

'So what do we tell them?' asked Puggy.

'Yachts—seabirds—tell them we're doing background shots for a children's series.'

There was nobody at the little alcove marked Reception. Victoria pinged the bell. A bare-legged girl in a white apron appeared briefly, muttered something in Spanish and disappeared. Maltravers watched Victoria becoming irritated. Her determination to look efficient always amused him. She was ringing the bell for the tenth time when the proprietress appeared from the rear part of the small pub-hotel. She apologised perfunctorily for staff shortages. She said Mr Weir was in the residents' lounge.

Sure enough, there he was in front of the television set, a glass of lager on the table beside his armchair, strong sunlight making it impossible to tell what programme he was watching, a youngish man with prematurely silver hair and a pale, smooth face.

'So you got my message from Jack Greeno?' he said.

'Yes,' said Victoria, looking round the little room, 'we had to hang about on the quay for what seemed like ages.'

'Why did we did have to come to this—'

'I'll show you your rooms upstairs,' said the landlady. Maltravers waited until they were in the sunny bedroom with the big double-bed and old-fashioned furniture.

'So what's the score, then?'

'You heard about the police sergeant?' Weir asked. 'Head beaten to a frazzle, great ox of a man he was—'

'Save it for the script.'

Puggy came into Jock's room and sat on one of the beds.

'I was telling Julian about the latest murder,' said Weir cheerfully. Maltravers did not think he was drunk. 'They came upon his mangled remains at the bottom of the old Roman bath, 'twas awful to behold—'

'Jock doesn't have conversations,' said Maltravers, 'he speaks dialogue. Without the Robert Newtons just what is the situation out there now? And why did we have to come all the way round the harbour to this quaint olde aleshoppe?'

'Greeno won't do the trip,' said Weir. 'He told me none of the Mundham boatmen will risk it. Anyway, he put me onto a guy here, you know his name? Quilt Bastable! They've searched the island twice—helicopter, dogs, the lot. They haven't found the old lady. They've left four or five flatfeet out there. From what I gather they think it was a local trying to rob the castle.'

'Just trying?' said Puggy. 'God help us when he gets serious.'

'So what've you fixed up with this boatman?'

Without knocking Victoria came into the little bedroom, eyes scanning their faces as though they might be conspiring to exclude her from something.

'His disposition is morose, tempered by occasional manifestations of surly avarice.'

'Greedy?'

'We're lucky he is. They've got a police launch out

there doing patrols. I had to agree to pay him a hundred quid, Julian.'

Puggy whistled. Victoria frowned.

'Oh well,' Maltravers began to say but Victoria quickly interrupted him.

'I'll talk to him about money,' she said.

'He wants it in advance.'

'I'm sure he does,' she drawled.

'Anyway, what I've arranged with him is we go out there tonight—tomorrow morning in the dark—then he'll pick us up again as soon as it's dark tomorrow night.'

'With coppers on the island and a bloody launch on patrol?' Puggy snorted.

'They're at the castle, it's a pretty big place, you won't be spotted if you stick to the interior and the far end—'

'What do you mean by *you*?' Victoria said.

'I didn't—'

'I like my writers to know what they're writing about,' she said snappily.

'Are you coming as well?' Maltravers asked, injecting a little mock surprise into his voice. It amused him to see Victoria's face redden.

'Why, did you think I'd stay here and wash your bloody drip-dry shirt?'

'Could be rough out there—for a woman,' Maltravers said, keeping the smile off his face.

Just in time she stopped herself from rising to his bait. She smirked.

'Perhaps I'm bringing out the mother in you, Julian.'

'I'm sorry for any helpless murderer who runs into this brittle band of backstabbers,' said Jock Weir quietly.

CHAPTER EIGHT

Daniels walked slowly across the former canteen hall which by the addition of some long trestle tables and telephones had been turned into their operations room.

'Llewellyn the librarian is on the line,' said Groves. 'Thank him for the map, the old windbag.'

He patted Daniels on the back. Daniels' mouth tightened momentarily. He picked up the phone on his desk in the little office. Wearily blinking he waited for the switchboard to put the call through. Four hours' sleep had not been enough.

'Ah, good morning—to whom am I speaking?' came the elderly librarian's surprisingly strong Welsh voice.

'Detective Inspector Daniels—we were going to phone you, Mr Llewellyn, great help that map. The Chief Constable will be writing to you.'

Groves grimaced.

'I like to be of help, Mr Daniels. Is Superintendent Groves available?'

'Is it urgent? He's rather—'

'I don't want to be a nuisance, a case like this must be an awesome responsibility for him...'

'Was there something else you wanted to bring up?' Daniels said gently, ignoring the faces Groves was pulling.

'Ah. Yes. Most emphatically. Was I bumbling on? Yes, something I heard from your people last night—no, the night before, wasn't it? Let me see, this is Saturday, yes, Thursday evening—'

Groves motioned urgently. Daniels put his palm over the mouthpiece.

'Can't you cut that old fool off?' Groves demanded. 'Does he want a medal for finding an old map?'

'Go on, Mr Llewellyn,' Daniels said, eyeing Groves calmly.

'—yes, I've been going through the old editions of the *Mundham Advertiser*, took me ages to find the bit I was looking for—I often think local newspapers only become interesting when they're turning yellow—like family snapshots.' Daniels realised he was expected to make a comment.

'That's very true.' He had never believed in excessive politeness—the only reason he went on listening so patiently was Groves' impatience.

'There was a case of trespass on Peacock Island in October nineteen-fifty-eight, Inspector,' Llewellyn said abruptly. 'I've got that issue of the *Advertiser* open in front of me. Do you want me to read it out?'

It was then that Groves picked up his phone.

'Put me onto the line Inspector Daniels is speaking on,' he growled. He looked at Daniels. 'I'll get rid of him for you.'

'I'm quite capable of handling it, thank you,' Daniels said. 'Go on, Mr Llewellyn.'

'This man was up before the bench on a summons alleging the attempted theft of two pheasants being the property of Lady Bennett. He pleaded not guilty—listen carefully—you're still there, are you?'

Daniels heard the clicking on the line as Groves' extension was connected.

'Yes, I'm listening.'

'He pleaded not guilty—he said he only landed on the island out of curiosity but two gardeners caught him and planted the two pheasants on his person. In a sack. I remembered this next bit from all these years ago,

68

Inspector, it came back to me when I heard the appalling details of Greeno's murder—this man, Sidney Marley, said he was attacked on the island by something that tried to tear out his eyes!'

Groves frowned.

'Tear out his eyes?' said Daniels.

'This is what he actually said: "Asked if he had anything to say on his own behalf the accused claimed he had landed on the island purely out of curiosity but was attacked by something that tried to tear out his eyes. The two gardeners chased it away and then lied to the police, saying he had the sack with the two pheasants when they caught him. He claimed he had never seen the sack before. The chairman, Major Humbleton, said he was sick and tired of defendants trying to wriggle out of well-justified retribution by slandering decent, law-abiding people. He imposed a fine of £50 or a month's imprisonment, with no time to pay".'

Groves' snort was heard on the line. He banged his phone down.

'Does it give an address for this Marley?' Daniels asked.

'Eighteen Old Quay Cottages. They're demolished now but Marley is a common name among the fishermen, Inspector, I'm sure he'll be well known.'

'Well, that is most interesting, Mr Llewellyn.'

'Bloody old nuisance,' Groves growled.

'I have that kind of memory, Inspector,' said Llewellyn. 'Some compensation for the onrush of old age. You are familiar with the curse of the island Keeper, Inspector? I detect from your accent that you're not a local man.'

'No, I—'

'Just old nonsense, of course, they had their jokers then as now.' His elderly, high-pitched voice took on a dramatic tone. 'Tread ye on this sacred dell the Bornless

69

Keeper ye shall see, Pointing the road to Hell. I hope I haven't been wasting your time, Inspector.'

He rang off abruptly, without saying goodbye. Daniels put down the phone. He decided to make no remark about Groves' behaviour. It would only lead to the taking up of postures, hostilities, the very kind of involvement he would never risk again.

'Curious coincidence?' he said calmly. 'Could be worth chasing up this man, Marley.'

Groves looked pained.

'This isn't Scotland Yard, you know,' he said, and the sneer was unmistakable. 'Waste valuable man-hours following up some bloody ragtail's yarn to get off a poaching charge? In nineteen-fifty-eight? You'll have to learn, Victor, a small town like this is full of cranks wanting to get in on the act. Now then—boats, that's the key to this case. None reported stolen, so our man must own one.'

'We're checking every boat we know about. But if it was an inflatable dinghy—you could keep it in a drawer. Or he could have towed it here on a trailer, slid it into the water at some quiet part of the harbour.'

'Just keep checking on boats,' said Groves, nodding wisely as though privy to secret knowledge. 'He's a local and somebody knows him and they're covering up for him.'

Groves' phone rang.

Daniels went out into the big room. He sat at a trestle table and looked down a list of names in his notebook, most of them already ticked off as having been contacted, boatmen, fishermen, yacht club employees, the captain of the Harbour Board dredger, an unofficial network of harbour worthies from whose eyes little could escape. He couldn't stop thinking of the name Sidney Marley.

A detective sergeant came across the big, bare room to

show him the latest progress on a list of local house-breakers, burglars and common thieves, all with a previous record of violence.

Two possibles had already been checked and found to have alibis: Carter, a Mundham fisherman who had two convictions for possessing stolen property, and a Beckham boatman called Bastable with a long history of petty thieving. The third outstanding candidate was serving two years in Exeter Gaol—as the sergeant said, the best alibi of all.

'Just check up with Exeter he isn't on their wonderful living-out rehabilitation scheme,' Daniels said. 'This Frowd chap, I remember him, one of my first cases here, remember him well, indecent assault, corruption of a minor, felonious assault—thieving was just a side-line to him.'

'That's him, threw a shoe at the Recorder last time he was in the dock.'

'Just check that he was cosy in his cell. A man who throws a shoe at a judge is capable of anything.'

The sergeant laughed. That's the second time in two days I've made a typical Groves-style remark, Daniels thought. The effect was dangerously pleasant. He sat back. Phones rang. Constables came and went. With a big case like this the lack of activity made him uneasy. But they had no leads. Until they got an inventory of the castle contents they couldn't tell if anything had been stolen, some identifiable antique perhaps that the murderer might offer to a dealer.

There were no fingerprints, no witnesses. The only positive trail the dogs had picked up on the first search had led straight into the water. As Groves said, it all pointed to a local with a boat, a man who knew the island well enough to lead Gould into the trap of the Roman bath.

He got up and walked over to the wall where they

71

had taped a blow-up of the island map. It didn't look much on paper but his feet knew how big it was. A mysterious sort of place. That tunnel through the rhododendron bushes had given him quite a spooky feeling, even in the company of two constables and a dog. As far as they knew no outsider had been allowed past the quay for at least ten years. Groves was working on the assumption that it was somebody who had been connected with the castle, old domestic staff perhaps. They had men tracing the old servants and gardeners now, those who were still alive.

Groves was probably correct, yet ... he stared at the map. There was something at the back of his mind, a slight nagging sensation, something he had heard or seen, something that wasn't right. He closed his eyes and tried to let his mind go blank. No, it wouldn't come, yet it went on irritating him.

He scratched his neck and made a note to get a haircut. He went through from the canteen annexe to the main building and spoke to the launch from the radio room. They had seen nothing. As he walked back he kept frowning. It all *seemed* very probable, the way Groves saw it, yet the more he thought about it the less certain he became. Groves was trying to force all the known facts into the simplest possible theory.

Why should it bother me, he asked himself. But he knew why. That pat on the back. The casual arrogance with which Groves had dismissed the librarian's phone call.

He made up his mind quickly. He would never have any peace if he allowed anybody to treat him as a doormat.

He went across the room to the smart young uniformed sergeant who was collating reports from the men who were checking the yacht club and Harbour Board moorings.

'Sergeant Butler,' he said quietly, 'I want to trace a man called Sidney Marley, last known address Eighteen Old Quay Cottages. He was up on a poaching charge a few years back.'

'Those cottages were demolished,' said Butler. 'The beat man would probably know, only we don't have beat men nowadays. I'll ask around.'

'No, don't ask around, put a man onto it. And tell me when you get anything.'

'Yes, sir,' said Butler. He watched Daniels walk away. As if it wasn't enough handling Grumpy Groves, now Mr Smartyboots Daniels was going to make a nuisance of himself. Plain-clothes men were all the same, big-headed prima donnas.

Like most members of the Mundham force he had been extremely curious as to why a crack Scotland Yard detective would suddenly decide to transfer to this sea-side backwater. Theories abounded. Some believed that all Metropolitan men were slightly bent and that Daniels had probably got out in advance of some scandal. Others thought his aloof manner concealed a raging ambition to get to the very top, which would be easier in a country force. A few thought he might have lost his nerve, dealing with all those London tearaways. Inevitably there were one or two who had London connections but the grapevine had no information on Daniels. His record was good, his promotions had come early, his marriage hadn't broken up, there wasn't even a sniff of corruption.

Of course nobody accepted the version Daniels had allowed to be put about, that Mundham was a better place to bring up kids. Detectives, it was universally accepted, didn't suffer from trivial family obligations.

Making a mental note to call Daniels 'sir' in future, just as a matter of politics, Butler picked up the phone

* * *

73

As Maltravers anticipated the boatman was now asking for more money. They met him in the rapidly filling saloon bar of the Red Lion. He was a surly-looking brute.

'I don't see the problem,' Victoria was saying. 'They've searched the island twice, they've only left a couple of men at the castle, they won't be going over the whole island again.'

'Guarantee that, can you?' growled Quilt Bastable, an unshaven man with yellow teeth. 'What about that launch they got out there patrollin'?'

Puggy had not been in favour of landing on the island.

'Even if they do nab you what's the most they can do —fine you a tenner for trespass?' he snapped at Bastable.

Maltravers smiled. What on earth *had* Victoria said to Puggy?

'It's not jist a question o' money,' Bastable growled, 'I got to live yere, police an' Harbour Master can be damn rough if they get a down on a boatman.'

Victoria's reaction surprised Maltravers. She shrugged and got to her feet.

'Sorry, a hundred's my top weight,' she said. 'Jock, better get in touch with that other boatman you saw—'

'All right,' Bastable said quickly, 'but you'll pay in advance?'

'You can have ten now and the rest when you bring us back.'

'Like hell—what if you git caught on the island?'

'I'll tell you what I'll do,' said Victoria, looking down at the boatman's darkly-lined face. 'We'll put the balance in an envelope and give it to the landlady here—we'll tell her it's a bet. If we get caught through no fault of yours you can have the money.'

'You don't trust me, is that it?'

74

'My mother warned me about trusting sailors. Are we on?'

'I dare say,' Bastable grunted.

'Come upstairs and I'll give you the money, Julian,' she said over her shoulder.

In her bedroom she was counting ten-pound notes from a man's wallet. Maltravers stood just inside the half-open door.

'You do the necessary,' she said, 'I'm going to have a bath before lunch.' She put the brown tenners on the bed. She began to unbutton her blouse. 'Did I handle him all right?'

'A lesson to us all, my sweet,' he said, picking up the notes and going back to the door. She pulled off the blouse, apparently indifferent to any interest he might show in her bare shoulders and inadequately covered breasts. 'Even Man the Brute seems to enjoy the delicate touch of the lady's whip.'

'But you're not that way inclined?'

Red hair fell, curtaining her face, as she started to unbuckle her fashionably wide leather belt. It was not often that Maltravers failed to have the last word. He shut the door. On his way down the stairs he told himself it was ridiculous but the fact was, she had succeeded —just for a moment—in arousing him. *Victoria?*

She looked at the closed door, standing in her blue bra and nylon panties. Perhaps that had been a mistake. Yet just for a moment she was certain his face had lost its normal air of mockery. She unhooked the bra and slipped off her panties. She looked at herself in the full-length wardrobe mirror. It'll take time, she thought, but you'll weaken, Julian, oh yes you will. And then we'll see who does the mocking...

Bastable's jaundiced eyes could hardly leave the white envelope with the nine brown tenners, now propped between two bottles of ginger wine on the top

75

shelf behind the bar. The landlady, of course, did not know how much was in the envelope.

'Mr Bastable is taking us out to film dawn breaking over the harbour,' said Maltravers. 'We'll be leaving very early, probably won't be back till midnight tomorrow.'

'Your young lady's already told me about the packed meals,' said the landlady.

'That's no young lady, that's our boss,' said Maltravers. When the landlady was out of earshot he grinned at Bastable and Puggy. 'If she didn't wear trousers I'd say no flies on our Victoria, eh?'

'Maybe she won't be so bloody cocky if she meets the bugger who bashed Big Gould's head in,' Bastable growled vindictively.

When the radio car reported that the envelope containing the will was not on the London train Groves' habitual air of secretiveness and superiority gave way to an outburst of temper. All that had happened was that the London solicitor's message-boy had missed the train at Waterloo and had put the envelope on the two-thirty instead.

'This is a murder investigation,' Groves shouted into the phone. 'The trouble with you people is you spend your lives with your noses stuck in bloody ledgers!'

It was one way of encouraging co-operation, Daniels thought.

'I'll just nip out and have a quick bite,' he said, leaving the small office before Groves could answer, even if he had heard through his slanging match with the London solicitor's clerk. He did not go to their usual café, Ye Brass Kettle, but headed towards Tucker Street. Marley had been quickly traced to Anstie House, a tall block of new council flats less than five minutes' walk from the station.

It did seem a little like misbehaving behind teacher's back, he thought as he started to climb five flights of stairs, the lift being out of action. Not that he was afraid of Groves but if Marley's yarn was a load of nonsense he did not want to give Alf the satisfaction of being right.

Calf muscles tight with the unusual exertion, and feeling sympathy for elderly council tenants who had to endure the council's chronically unreliable lifts, he knocked at number seventeen. He'd read the file on Sidney Marley: petty thieving, taking boats without owners' consent, the poaching conviction; more unusual, an anonymous letter stating categorically that he was having incestuous relations with both his daughters. No action had been taken although both girls had been interviewed.

Nothing in that little lot that would disqualify him from being Citizen of the Year in this town, Daniels thought, hearing the vibrations of heavy feet. The door opened.

'Sidney Marley?'

'I'm not buyin' nothin',' the man growled. He was about sixty, grey-haired, unshaven. He wore a thick cotton shirt without a collar. Braces held up war-surplus trousers and on his feet were what must have been slippers, once.

'Police,' said Daniels quietly. 'I'd like a chat.'

'Oh yeah?' Marley left the door open. Daniels shut it behind him and went into a small living-room. Marley was turning down the volume of the television set. He had been watching a children's programme.

'My name's Daniels.'

'Oh yeah?'

Daniels felt too brisk and well-dressed for these

cramped, shabby surroundings. Marley sat in his TV chair. A perfunctory hand gesture might have been an invitation for Daniels to join a pile of newspapers and a black and white cat on a sagging sofa. He remained standing.

'You've heard about these murders on Peacock?' he said.

'Would be hard not to. What's it got to do wi' me, then?'

As he spoke Marley kept his eyes on the silent TV picture.

'You were caught poaching out there, about twelve years ago. I was interested in that.'

'Was you? My back's so bad I can hardly bend down to tie me shoes. You think I'm likely to be out on that effin' island smashin' Big Gould's head in?'

'You told the beak the gardeners planted those pheasants on you—and that something tried to attack you—tear out your eyes, you told the court.'

Marley sniffed. Looking at his unshaven profile and then at the eyes steadily concentrating on the screen, Daniels found himself making a mental note of the man's interest in children. One of his previous convictions was for stealing brass fittings while employed as a boilerman at Carter Street secondary school. Not forgetting the anonymous letter. It was the sort of information a small-town detective stored away over the years. Daniels wondered how long he'd have to serve in Mundham before he knew all of the inhabitants and their secrets. He wished he didn't have to know *any*.

'You did tell the beak something tried to tear out your eyes, didn't you?'

'All lies, the beak said. Humbleton—a right bastard. Fifty quid, no time to pay. Where's I to get fifty quid? I did a month in Dorchester for that.'

'But what was it attacked you?'

'It was jist a tale I gave the beak.'

'I don't believe you.'

'Oh yeah? I don't remember that far back anyways.'

'I don't believe you.'

'There you are, then.'

Daniels turned to the window. Down below in the street some children were climbing in and out of a car. It was a brilliantly warm day. Outside.

'This your own place, is it?' he asked, without looking round.

'More or less.'

'One of your daughters putting you up, is she?'

'What's that to do wi' it?'

A boy wrestled one of the smaller children to the pavement, sitting astride his chest, pinning down his wrists. Two passing workmen ignored the children.

'Council's very strict on keeping lodgers,' Daniels said quietly. 'Pets as well, you have to have written permission, I hear they don't give it easily.'

'You're all the same, you lot. Effin' coppers.'

'Just tell me what happened, on the island.'

It wasn't much of a threat but it worked with Marley. Perhaps he'd had experience of police threats, Daniels thought. What a small-town force like this lacked in brain-power it made up in knowing how to put the squeeze on its locals.

Marley had landed on Peacock Island from curiosity, sure enough, curiosity as to what he could steal.

'I'm up top, scoutin' round like—the birds niver gets shot at so you can catch 'em easy enough—then it jumps me from the back.'

'What jumps you?'

Marley poked a thick index finger in his ear and twisted it about. He took his eyes off the screen long enough to examine the haul of wax.

'I should niver've told the beak, he put me away for

79

four weeks on account of tellin' him—if I'd said guilty he'd've given me a fiver fine. Nobody believed it an' I niver told a single soul else, till now.'

'What was it?'

'It jumped on me back, I started shoutin' with the shock, all I know is it had claws, big uns, they was tryin' to tear at me eyes, I was wrestlin' wi' it, good job I was strong in them days—as it was it got me half down—'

'What kind of claws?'

'Big, flashin' in front of my face. You know, claws, dark and shiny.'

'Like a bird's?'

'Could be. Anyway, these two old gardeners come runnin' and they hit it off wi' their rakes—then they take me to the castle and Lady Bennett tells 'em what to do, next thing they're givin' me to the police and handin' over this bag wi' the two pheasants—I niver saw them birds till then!'

'Well, what was this thing with the claws?'

'It was strong—I think there was feathers but it didn't feel like no bird—more like a monkey maybe. It had a fair grip on me, I'll tell you that.'

'Did the gardeners say anything? Or the old lady?'

'No, they was confabbin' togither for a bit then she phones the police—'

'There's no phone.'

'There was then, she niver paid no bills after she turned peculiar, they took it out. Jack Greeno told me that. I did ask the gardeners what it was, they both said they niver saw a bloody thing, lyin' old gits.'

'Why did you think it might be a monkey?'

'I dunno, the way it jumped up on me back—I mean, people keep them monkeys as pets, don't they? She was a great one for animals, Lady Bennett.'

'But you never actually saw it?'

'No, I was halfways to the ground and they come

runnin'. I suppose it was off into the bushes.' They heard a key turning in the front door. 'I should've niver opened my bloody mouth about it, that's why Major effin' Humbleton give me four weeks in Dorchester.'

'You there, Dad?' came a woman's voice.

'In here,' Marley called.

'I'll be going, then,' said Daniels. 'Keep this to yourself and we won't be bothering you again.'

'Oh yeah?'

The woman came into the small living-room. She took one look at Daniels and turned accusingly on her father.

'You in bother with the police again?' she demanded.

'Just chatting,' said Daniels.

When he came out of the front entrance a small boy of about four was wriggling head-first through the jagged space of the abandoned car's windscreen. Daniels passed without speaking.

Groves was getting ready to leave for the island as soon as the two-thirty from London arrived with the will.

'Had a leisurely snack?' he said sarcastically. 'While you were gone we've had one bit of luck. They've traced Lady Bennett's last boatman, his name's Len World, he's in the geriatric ward at Little Whittenham. The matron says he's lucid enough only he isn't too sure what year he's living in, lucky bugger.'

'You want me to go out there and see him?'

'There were a lot of people on Peacock at one time, he'll know all their family histories. We're looking for somebody who knew that island well. Come out to the castle when you get back, it'll be an all-night job.'

'Might be worth while taking camp beds out there.'

Groves patted him on the shoulder.

'It's what you must expect on a big case like this,' he said patronisingly. To the best of Daniels' knowledge this was only the second murder inquiry Groves had worked on in twenty years. He said nothing about Sidney Marley.

As he drove out of the car-park for Little Whittenham he tried to let his mind go blank. Something was still nagging at him. He was so busy thinking he forgot that the town's expensive new traffic consultant had devised a brilliant one-way system for the Sturminster Road roundabout.

He had to reverse the Rover twenty yards back into Winifrith Street before he could pick up the correct lane for entering the roundabout system. He began to go over everything Marley had told him. Those claws ... Barham had been strong on claws at first, although he wasn't saying much about them now Alf was back ... suppose the old lady had been keeping something like that as a pet, a chimp maybe ...

He could well imagine what Groves' reaction would be to the theory that they were looking for a man-killing monkey.

CHAPTER NINE

It was four in the morning when they came blearily down the darkened stairs of the Red Lion and crossed the quayside parking space to the blue Peugeot. Jock Weir directed Maltravers to Bastable's moorings, a concrete jetty built by the Army for wartime amphibious training, now derelict. On their way down a bumpy track the headlights picked out clumps of scraggy bushes and the skeletons of army huts.

Bastable untied the big open boat and they slipped

away from the quay. A mist made it impossible to see any stars, although the moon was palely visible, a fuzzy yellow blob in the southern sky. Bastable was not given to easy small-talk but Puggy did extract the disturbing information that he was steering by what to them were the barely discernible lights of harbour buoys.

The four of them sat among the equipment, cigarette ends throwing a red glow on cheeks and noses.

'You can say goodbye to any filming if this fog keeps up,' said Puggy.

'Sea mist, that's all, get a lot of them in summer,' said Maltravers. 'It'll evaporate in the blazing sun—'

'Blazing policemen more like,' said Jock. 'I feel awful. Was D-Day like this, Puggy?'

'Less risky but we weren't being paid so well.'

They felt the boat rolling slightly as Bastable closed down the engine. They presumed they were nearing the island.

'I always wanted to be a cockleshell hero,' said Jock. 'Shouldn't we have blackened our faces?'

Bastable heard the police launch and hissed at them to keep down. For a few moments it seemed to be coming directly towards them, spotlight beam cutting through the mist. Then it began to turn, the long cone of light picking out rocks and bushes. The water was like ink.

As soon as the beam was out of sight Bastable opened the throttle a fraction and almost soundlessly the boat moved in towards the black bulk of Peacock Island. A faint jar told them when the nose was touching land.

In gumboots borrowed from Bastable, at no extra charge, Puggy and Maltravers climbed over the prow, stretching their legs down into the gently lapping water. They found themselves standing in hard shingle. In the dark Victoria could not be sure which of them took her in his arms and carried her a few paces up the sloping beach. She hoped it was Maltravers.

She waited as shadowy figures carried the equipment onto dry land, the big camera case, the shoulder harness, the hold-all with cans of unexposed film stock, the other bags with packed lunches and bottles of beer.

Puggy gave Jock a piggy-back while Maltravers stood in six inches of water, hands on the side of the boat.

'Ten-thirty tonight, then,' he said to Bastable, who had made no offer to help with the unloading. 'We'll wait up in the trees until we see your light.'

'Be sharp then, I can't be hangin' around here.'

'And if anyone wants to know where we are, say I met a yacht-owner who's taking us round the coast.'

'I won't be speakin' to nobody.'

With a shove from Maltravers the boat moved slowly off the shingle and then disappeared into the misty blackness. They picked up the big camera case and the bags and made their way carefully up the short stretch of open beach into the shelter of bushes which they could feel against their faces but hardly see.

Shielding the torch with his body Maltravers made sure they had left nothing on the exposed beach. They squatted down to wait for first light. They heard the police launch again and flattened themselves as brilliant light flooded the branches above.

As soon as they were in darkness again Maltravers felt in the hold-all.

'What are you doing?' Victoria demanded when she heard the cap of the whisky bottle being unscrewed.

'I always have a stiff scotch to help me through day-break,' came the mocking voice of Maltravers. 'You want some?'

'I do,' said Jock quickly, 'a large tot before we go over the top.'

'I should have thought you had enough last night,' said Victoria sharply. 'Nervous, are you?'

'Who, me?' said Jock. 'Not at all, I often crawl out of bed before dawn to creep about strange islands inhabited only by bloodthirsty maniacs. Want some, Puggy?'

'No.'

'At least Puggy isn't a dipso or a nervous nellie,' said Victoria icily. It was the first personal remark she'd made to him since they'd left London, Puggy thought. He knew what a strain she was under. If he could have been sure of not grasping the wrong hand he would have stretched out in the dark to give her a reassuring squeeze.

As he slipped the bottle back into the bag Maltravers thought it might have been a mistake to let Jock know about the whisky. The day ahead would be fairly boring for him and Victoria. At least he hoped it was going to be boring for Victoria; if she was going to make a nuisance of herself interfering with the filming the whole thing would become impossible.

From higher up on the dense slopes they heard an owl hooting.

'This appeals to my sense of the ridiculous,' said Jock.

'It isn't ridiculous!' Victoria's voice was becoming edgy.

'Nothing's ridiculous if you're making money at it,' said Puggy.

'Oh, that's what you're doing, is it?' Maltravers said, mockingly.

'What the hell was that?' Groves snarled, grabbing Daniels' arm, his other hand raising the claw hammer to strike into the shadows on the great stairway.

'A rat,' said Daniels, putting his hand over his mouth to silence an involuntary yawn. It would have sounded like a sarcastic comment. It was almost five o'clock and his eyes were sore.

They had spent the whole night going from room to room, checking those contents of the castle against the inventory stapled to their copy of Lady Bennett's will. Nothing was missing so far but they had another three foolscap sheets to work through, a separate list of stuff from a house the Bennetts had owned in Somerset. They presumed this was in the crates which were lying about all over the place, obviously standing exactly where the haulage removers had dumped them ten years before.

Groves was insisting they prise open each heavy wooden box. Daniels suspected that Groves was hoping to find Lady Bennett's body stuffed in with the china and gilt-framed pictures and dusty bric-à-brac. It was clear the Bennetts had not gone in for valuable antiques, no silver, no ornate duelling-pistols or first editions. Millionaires or not, they seemed to have had a liking for good old-fashioned junk. It was also clear that Groves was becoming edgy.

'Where are those buggers?' he demanded, looking over the banisters. 'Come on, you lot, get up here and lend a hand with these bloody crates.'

As wood cracked and nails screeched Groves became more and more irritable. His overnight dash from Wales was now beginning to look foolish. Under the crumpled newspapers on top of the tenth and last crate there was no body, only pots and pans. Groves swore.

'I'm going out for a breather,' said Daniels.

He stood on the front steps of the castle. The dawn was soft and misty, a pink light spreading high from the east. Tired as he was it still nagged at him, whatever it was. The trouble was that with Groves around he couldn't concentrate. Any detective knew that to get the brain really working it had to be your own case, you couldn't share it. The sixth sense needed lots of elbow-room. He stretched his arms and shrugged. He was glad to have all that behind him.

'I've let them get on with checking the lists,' said Groves, appearing beside him. He sounded resentful.

'Doesn't look as if anything's been stolen.'

'That doesn't mean the intention wasn't there.' Groves got out his cigarettes. Suddenly he snapped his fingers. 'Unless—cash! Why didn't—'

'I did think of that,' Daniels said. 'She hasn't been off the island for ten years or more, we know Turle Greeno only cashed an occasional cheque for her in the town, twenty pounds at most, and if she'd had it from before she turned dotty it wouldn't be legal tender, considering how often we've changed our bank-notes.'

'She could've got it by post,' Groves said, without conviction.

'I asked Putnam the water postman. He doesn't remember any registered mail. We could check with the bank's head office—and her solicitors.'

'Why didn't you?'

'I've been on this island most of the time,' Daniels said, intending nothing more than a statement of fact. Groves didn't take it that way. Without looking at him Daniels sensed that he was becoming angry.

'This old fellow you saw last night at the hospital— you didn't get *anything* from him?'

'Not really. He kept saying he knew about the three murders. I couldn't get him to understand we didn't know for sure that Lady Bennett is dead. Nice old chap, shame to think they end up in places like that, all those old men, bald as eggshells most of them, dribbling and—'

'I don't want to hear all that crap! Didn't he suggest a name, somebody who knew the island? Somebody with a grudge against her, somebody she sacked?'

'No. He didn't.'

'You did ask him. I take it?'

Daniels said nothing. Groves had wanted all the credit, it was his own fault if he now looked like falling on his face.

'Let's take a stroll round the grounds,' Groves said, 'I think I'm getting a bit bloody neurotic in that mausoleum.'

Daniels assumed this was some kind of apology. It made no difference to him.

They turned the corner of the castle and walked slowly towards the church.

'That's where the dog took us,' Daniels said, pointing to the tumbled gap in the graveyard wall. 'Right to Sir Godfrey's grave he went.'

Groves followed him into the long grass. Their feet were damp after a couple of steps. There was a certain suspense about Groves' silence, as though he was working himself up to some kind of outburst. Daniels hoped he wouldn't. Dew-drops were strung like pearls on a spider's solitary strand.

'I haven't seen that since I was a boy on the farm,' said Groves, looking down into the grass. White maggots flowed like lava through the hollowed-out belly of a dead hedgehog. Daniels grimaced.

'I didn't fancy breakfast anyway.'

'Nothing revolting about it,' Groves said, the tension gone from his voice. 'It's Nature's way of disposal, the never-ending cycle. That's what I should've been but there was no money in the family.'

'No money for what?'

'I wanted to be a vet or a marine biologist—something to do with animals. I ended up studying people instead. What was it you really wanted to be, Victor?'

'Strange as it may seem I never wanted to be anything else but a detective.' Groves' unexpected little intimacies must have been contagious. 'So we both ended up in the wrong job,' he said, almost sadly.

'Is that why you left London? I often wondered. Thought you'd just quietly drift towards your pension in this backwater?'

'Not exactly, no, I—'

Groves nodded sympathetically.

'Oh well, there's a lot of people who'd be a lot happier if they'd face up to the fact that they're failures,' he said.

Daniels stared at him venomously.

'Who said I was—' he stopped himself. 'Over here,' he said abruptly.

'Fancy bit of marble Sir Godfrey got for himself,' Groves said, looking down at the head of the marble warrior. 'Great thing about the rich, they'll spend a fortune on gravestones for themselves but not a penny to keep some poor beggar alive. You ever notice, in these old country graveyards, half the stones are for little children? The rich man in his castle ...'

Daniels stared down at the stone. Was it his own fault? But how could he have explained it to men like Groves? He would never understand. What did a bumptious dunderhead like him know about—

'You say the dog was interested in this?' Groves was saying, one hand on the marble knight's shoulder, the other feeling down the side of the massive block. Daniels watched coldly as he squatted on his haunches, fingers tracing a line along the stone.

'Is that what you think?' Daniels demanded. 'Is it?'

'Yeah,' said Groves slowly. He rose and walked round the stone, bent almost double. Then he straightened up. He looked triumphant. 'This thing's designed to move,' he said.

'Nonsense,' Daniels snapped, 'it must weigh a ton, a block of marble this size.'

'Ah—but look, it isn't a block of marble, is it?'

'What do you mean?'

'The marble only goes down an inch or so—look, there's the crack—it's just a lid on top of this stone base.'

'Congratulations,' Daniels said, but Groves was not listening. Unwillingly Daniels found himself becoming curious as to what was making him so enthusiastic. He took a hesitant step nearer the stone.

'Look,' said Groves, 'the marble's resting on the stone, you can see the line—but see how it's cut? Come up this end. Look! It's only resting solid in the middle. It's the same on the other side. See how the crack gets wider at the ends! It's designed to swivel.'

Ridiculous as the idea was and still fuming at Groves' remark about being a failure, Daniels' curiosity triumphed. Grunting a little, the two detectives put their hands on the marble arm. Arching their backs, toes sliding on grass, they began to push. The block felt immovable. Daniels stood up, rubbing the small of his back.

'A lot of people would be happier if they just admitted it,' he said, feeling a little cheerier. Groves was an idiot.

'Try it at the other end,' said Groves.

Daniels snorted. Groves was bustling about now like a man possessed. He placed both palms on the warrior's cold feet.

'You'll develop good muscles,' Daniels said. 'If you—'

Groves hardly began to exert full pressure. With a gentle scraping sound the warrior began to swing away from him. He went on pushing until the shallow marble cover was lying diagonally across the space it had been sealing. Daniels looked down into a stone trench, about four feet deep, most of it occupied by a fungus-encrusted coffin.

Groves was already halfway into the trench. The wood

of the coffin was soft and rotten. His fingers probed at the lid. It lifted easily.

They dragged it clear and dropped it on the grass. An explosive smell erupted in their faces. They stood over the exposed coffin. They were looking at the outline of a human figure wrapped in a heavy brocade bedcover.

Groves got both feet into the trench, sitting on the edge of the stone base. He tugged at a corner of the bedcover. It came away with a jerk.

They saw a silvery head of woman's hair and a skeleton face.

'Lady Bennett, I presume,' Daniels said quietly. Groves was smiling and nodding his head.

'I told you, didn't I?' he said. 'Only a local would know about this. I told you so all along.'

Daniels felt words choking in his throat. A chance remark and this little bit of luck and Groves had made him look like a failure. What was worse, he even *felt* like a failure.

It was no consolation to see that this ignorant oaf had no idea what his discovery meant.

The harsh screech echoed round the gentle slope of the wide clearing. High above in a blue sky seagulls glided effortlessly on air currents but down here there was no breeze.

Puggy lay on his stomach beside a yellow blaze of gorse. The next screech came from only a few feet away. Round the gorse thicket came a peacock's head. A tilted eye stared down at the camera.

Just then, from among the taller pines on the far side of the clearing, down the short bank of what local myth said was the sacred mound, came the shrouded figure of a monk, face hidden in the dark shroud of a black cowl.

It was walking slowly, arms folded in voluminous sleeves, walking in a direct line towards Puggy.

CHAPTER TEN

'Shoo! Piss off!'

Puggy chucked a handful of dirt at the peacock's craning neck. The bird drew back quickly, mottled tail feathers rustling on grass. Puggy got his eye back to the viewfinder, easing the big Arriflex camera back against his shoulder.

The monk was still coming towards him. Puggy took his face away from the viewfinder and waved his left arm. The monk stopped and went back up the slope into the pines.

A few seconds later the same black figure reappeared in the viewfinder. A faint whirring noise came from the camera magazine. The monk came right up to him.

'What happened the first time?' Maltravers asked, pulling the cowl off his blond head and kneeling beside the cameraman.

'A bloody peacock came right across vision.'

'Lovely birds but evil-spirited. Odd that nature should combine such elegance with those revolting vocal chords.'

'I've known women like that.' Puggy checked what was left on the 400-foot roll. 'We've shot seven and a half minutes—gives you another three and a half minutes on this one. You don't want to use more footage on this monk gimmick, do you?'

'Victoria's very words.'

'We're not even sure it's historically accurate.'

'How pedantic. A religious hermit lived here before William the Conqueror. Who's to say what gear he actually wore? Victoria didn't like the idea because she didn't think of it herself.'

'I think it's a lot of bollocks, personally.'

'It's a nice image. We've got to show something moving, create atmosphere. If I had a bottle of tomato sauce I might even suggest stunting up a mangled corpse.'

'I'm sure you would. Where now?'

'The Roman bath, I think. That'll give us some footage on the actual murders.'

'I'm starving.'

'Let's do the bath first.' He snapped his fingers. 'Shit! I forgot to hide that bottle of scotch.'

'You think Victoria's likely to allow Jock to start swilling whisky?'

'You see her as a strict disciplinarian, eh?' He smiled lewdly.

'I don't see life through kinky-tinted spectacles,' Puggy said, defensively.

'You miss half the fun, old chap.'

Maltravers took off the monk's robe and folded it up.

'We'll pick it up on the way back,' he said, shoving it under the gorse.

'Part of your kinky wardrobe, is it?'

Maltravers winked.

Taking care to stay in the shelter of trees and bushes they started down into the heart of the island. Myriads of small birds scattered before them. Rabbits bolted into thick undergrowth. They saw what Puggy maintained were smoothly worn badger paths. Even he, the keen gardener, could not put a name to some of the flowering bushes. Over the decades the island's various owners had taken advantage of its sheltered, luscious climate to import flowers and shrubs from many parts of the world. Maltravers listened indifferently to

Puggy's attempts to identify exotic blossoms. The idea of *naming* flowers bored him stiff. Did Puggy know what void he was trying to fill with his gardening and his fishing and all the other cosy little hobbies? The whole place was overheated and too lushly brilliant by far. At times they walked through sun-dappled tunnels formed by plumes of ferns much taller than a man. And never far away, the most striking feature of all, the opulent blue of the peacocks, strutting and rustling through small clearings. The incessant screams of the cocks, harsh and arbitrarily timed, seemed to convey a message of raging grievance.

Maltravers picked his way down a short, steep slope, using the gnarled, exposed roots as steps.

'There should be a path down here, Lover's Walk it was called.'

'I thought nobody was allowed on this island,' said Puggy, moving easily despite the bulk of the camera.

'My old man knew the late Sir Godfrey Bennett, they were both directors of a mining outfit in South America —making fortunes out of slave labour to be exact. The old man did a lot of sailing along this coast, we came here quite a bit. The Bennetts were stinking rich—I mean, we were only averagely well-off.'

'Poor bastards.'

'They lived in the grand manner, butlers, footmen, cooks, gardeners, boatmen, maids—ah yes, the maids.'

'You were screwing one, were you?'

'You can be very coarse.' It did strike him as rather strange, the change in Puggy's manner, as if the weight of thirty pounds of camera round his shoulders was necessary to put him in harmony with the world. Or maybe it was because he was out of Victoria's orbit. 'I had a boyish romance with one of the maids. Dear Thelma, where art thou now?'

'How old were you?'

'Fourteen—fifteen, I was mature for my age—it goes with money. I used to slip away in a dinghy. Ah yes, many a ripe afternoon we whiled away in innocent, childish merriment—up in the ferns!'

'I didn't realise you had such an over-privileged youth. I was apprenticed at fourteen.'

'You didn't realise I ever showed much interest in girls was what you were thinking.'

'I didn't say that.'

'No, you didn't ... tactful bastard ... I'm a strange case, if I say so myself. That was the only time in my life I've really been in love. Thelma—the older I get the more I think of her. I even thought of tracing her— but she'll be fat and fortyish, married to some decent yokel ... probably forgotten all about me.'

'I *married* my childhood sweetheart. There's no nostalgia.'

'Come on, it must be satisfying, fatherhood, creating a family, all that crap?'

'You ought to try it, Julian.'

'Don't you think I'd like to?'

'It's easy enough. Too bloody easy ...'

'Freedom, is that what you're sickening after? It's an illusion. Look at me, free as the birds in the tree ... and lonely as the ...'

They walked on in silence. Maltravers suddenly stopped and faced the cameraman.

'You don't want to throw it all away, Puggy. She isn't worth it.'

'Who isn't worth what?'

'You know. Look, Puggy, just while we're having this moment of—'

'I don't think we should talk about it.'

'Sorry. None of my business.'

They skirted the blue waters of the claypool and started down the slope towards the north side of the island. When Puggy spoke his voice was low and intense.

'I just can't help myself. What the hell am I going to do? Quite a lot of the time I wish I was dead.'

Maltravers winced. Puggy was not joking.

'Surely you could have a bit on the side, plenty of stray women about—'

'She despises me, doesn't she?'

Hesitating a fraction too long, Maltravers tried to sound cheerful:

'She despises all men, that's what makes her type tick, the urge to prove she's better than—'

'She doesn't despise you.'

'Ah—but I'm the current competition, don't you see? She beat me for the job—but can she see me off properly? Ah ha! That's what's eating into her.'

'While to you it's just a game, eh? Or so you pretend.'

'All right, it is a game but I'm not one of your gentleman amateurs, old chap, I play to win. You know something, it makes me almost physically sick to lose—at anything, even shove ha'penny in a pub. And no bloody woman ...' his voice trailed off. Trouble about naïve, earnest people like Puggy, they got you at it, spouting embarrassing nonsense ...

Standing by the black trunk of a chestnut tree heavy with white candles they looked down a slope and across the path. Beyond stretched a flat waste of reedy ground dotted with bushes. Mundham's quays were visible across the water.

'Give it a minute, make sure there's no cops nosing around,' Maltravers murmured. He looked sideways at Puggy. It was obvious he hadn't liked the turn the conversation had taken. It would be interesting to see if Puggy told her what he had said. The poor dope was probably having an inner struggle over loyalties.

They slid down the embankment and crossed the path. The police had cleared the surrounds of the

Roman bath. Puggy walked twice round the sunken walls and then took up a position from where he could track in from the harbour panorama to the bath and then down to where the mould-covered floor was darkly red.

Maltravers kept a watch along the path.

He did not look back up the slope. The feathered creature was behind the chestnut tree, the bright eyes in the deep sockets watching their every movement. Then it glided away. It would be easier to start with the red-haired woman and the other man.

By the time they got off the launch that brought them and Lady Bennett's body back to the town quays Groves was on top of the world. His face was grim as they moved through the crowds of gaping holidaymakers and jostling cameramen. He said nothing to the running straggle of reporters. But he was a happy man.

'This has narrowed it right down,' he said, twice, in the car. Daniels said nothing.

When they were alone in the small office Groves leaned back on the window-sill. He should have had a waistcoat to stick his thumbs in, Daniels thought, so full of himself as he now was.

'Basically I've got the picture,' he said, or declaimed. 'Our man knows the island intimately. He twigs there's something wrong with Lady Bennett. He goes out there and finds her dead. He decides to hide the body. He's clever, a grave is the last place we'd look. Greeno turns up, recognises him, he panics. Maybe we'll charge him with Lady Bennett's murder, he thinks. So he kills Greeno. He can't leave the island till it's dark so he hides in the trees. Maybe he's waiting for a chance to get back into the castle. Bob Gould spots him. He recognises him as well. So he lets Bob chase him to the Roman bath, Bob falls in, he bashes Bob's head to a

97

pulp. So what've we got? I'll tell you. A local thief who knows the island backwards—'

'And is also a savage maniac?' said Daniels calmly.

'Oh yeah, he's a nut into the bargain. Now then, what does my experience tell me about that kind of nutter? I'll tell you. They build up to it gradually, then one day—bingo—they explode. So—let's start looking back —any local with a record of irrational violence, I don't know, cruelty to animals maybe. Remember that lout who was firing arrows into cows up on Claiborne Hill? Anything that looks the slightest bit kinky. All right?'

'I'll start checking,' said Daniels. He didn't move.

'Well?'

'You don't think we're narrowing it down too much? We're only presuming the motive was theft. I don't know if—'

'When you make up your mind give me first refusal,' said Groves. 'Meanwhile let's have some bloody action about here.'

Daniels looked at him impassively. Then he went out into the big room. An hour later Barham came on the line. His post-mortem showed that Lady Bennett had died of a heart attack, about five days before. The rats had attacked her after death. Groves saw no sense in wondering why the thief *then* decided to hide her body. Or why he hadn't bothered to hide Greeno's body.

'He could have been there for days threatening her with violence to make her tell him where the valuables were. That would bring on a heart attack. Maybe he had to leave her—he might have a job, could only get back at the weekends. He hides her body. Greeno arrives. He does for Greeno but he hasn't time to hide the body, he doesn't know that Jack is going to do another trip before he bothers to look for Turle. Anyway, he isn't rational. When is that fingerprint man to tell us whose prints are on the gravestone, that's what I want to bloody know.'

Daniels sat at the other desk, ostensibly waiting for the records sergeant to come up with a list of local perverts. It was not too difficult to shut Groves' voice out when you concentrated hard enough. Where was he going to start? No ordinary thief would have bothered to hide Lady Bennett's body in the same coffin as the skeleton of her dead husband. Why hide her body and not the other two? Why kill one by slashing his throat and the other by bashing his head in? Rats could not have got at the old lady in the coffin. *Bashing his head in?*

He chewed his lower lip, staring at the scatter of paper on his desk.

'What's on your mind?' Groves asked, suspicious as always.

'It just occurred to me,' Daniels said casually, 'I wonder what happened to Gould's helmet?'

'His *helmet*? Is that what you're pondering? Jesus Christ, man, I—'

'We didn't find it, did we? You think maybe your thief took it as a memento?'

'Well, if that's all you can . . .'

Daniels was no longer listening. Motive, that was the key. His fingers patted the various sheets of paper.

Then he found it. Sheets of heavy foolscap, legal paper, the bottom five pages still folded over from last night in the castle.

He turned them over until the three pages bearing the photostat of the will were on top. The headed paper belonged to the London solicitors. The will was dated January 1956. The usual legal wording, being of sound mind . . . Lady Margot Bennett, née Margot Cavendish, widow of the late Sir Godfrey Bennett . . . his eyes tracked through the legal verbiage . . . I hereby bequeath the property known as Peacock Island in the Harbour of Mundham ... all fixtures and contents and appurtenances as hereinafter listed ... all monies, bills, shares ... and then he came to the name.

Groves was now on the phone, asking someone if, by any chance, not that it really mattered, anyone had come across Sergeant Gould's helmet.

Daniels reached for his own phone and asked the switchboard girl to get him Kenworthy, Kenworthy, Frowd, solicitors of Chancery Lane, London E.C.4.

He kept his voice down. Groves could get on with his own theory. Groves was a fool. No stray thief would commit two murders for the sake of the junk in that castle. But what better motive was there for murder than a million pounds? And who more likely to know about a trick gravestone than a member of the family?

A *failure*? They could have imagined anything else about him and he wouldn't have given a damn. But not *that*. It was ludicrous but it was the worst insult of all, the one thing that could have brought back to life the man he used to be.

'We have four men at the castle and the launch is making sure nobody lands,' Groves was saying on the phone. 'No—of course the bloody press aren't allowed on the island! I don't care, I don't give a fart where they come from, they go near Peacock Island and I'll have their guts for garters ... tell them anything you like ... no, don't tell them *that*, if they think he's still out there they'll be hiring every boat in the habour ... he may be a homicidal maniac but he had enough sense to get well clear before we turned up with teams of dogs!'

He slammed down the phone.

CHAPTER ELEVEN

It was very hot. Maltravers lay on his stomach, propped on his elbows, looking straight into the creamy swell of Victoria's thinly-covered breasts. He was reading to her from notes scribbled on the back of an envelope. She was printing the details of what they had shot on the labels of the film cans and then into her notebook. To go with her red hair she had fair skin heavy with freckles, especially about her shoulders and chest. She had undone most of the buttons of her cardigan. Her bra was light blue, with half cups that hardly seemed adequate.

Maltravers had no doubt he was being given this close-up deliberately. Unexpectedly, it was exciting him.

'This monk stuff, it's too damn gimmicky,' she said.

'Gives us a bit of atmosphere—we'll do well with it on the Continent, juicy murders, exotic blossoms, the grim cowl of the black monk—all good kinky stuff. They'll love it in Germany.'

'We'll see what it looks like,' she said, dismissively.

'This place gives me the creeps without any kinky gimmicks,' said Jock Weir.

Maltravers looked over his shoulder. Puggy was sitting against a tree-trunk, staring out over the harbour, the *Angling Times* on his lap. Jock was on his back, eyes closed, hand occasionally lifting to sweep insects off his face.

The spot they had chosen as a kind of base was almost at the top of the northern slope of the island, a little plateau screened on both sides by banks of ferns. The tops of small trees and bushes growing precariously on the steep drop shielded them from the police launch that passed round the island every fifteen minutes or so.

From here, across the rich blue of the harbour expanse, they could see the buildings on Mundham's quay-fronts. Occasionally a boatload of sightseers would make a wide sweep of the island and they could hear the booming voices of the boatmen's commentaries. Maltravers felt unusually tense.

'Peacock Island has romantic connotations for me,' he said quietly, looking at Victoria's breasts.

'Really?' she said, still writing in her notebook.

'It was here I lost my—what's that word? Oh yes, I remember, innocence.'

'How utterly fascinating. I wouldn't have thought you ever had any to lose. Five-year-old, were you?'

'Surprises me as well, sweetness. I wonder if I could find the actual spot. Who knows, confrontation with the past might be illuminating.'

She showed no reaction. He rose slowly to his feet.

'I won't be ten minutes,' he said to Puggy. 'Then we'll do the clay-pool.'

'I don't think we've really got time to waste on sentimental explorations, Julian,' she said sharply.

He stood over her. For such a brittle woman her breasts really were fulsome. It was a long time since he had thought about *breasts*.

'Is that an order?' he asked.

She looked up, pulling red hair off her eyes.

'Do you take orders?' she asked.

'No.'

He had almost reached the ferns when he heard her voice.

'It's time I saw some of the beauty spots,' she said, her voice heavily casual. 'We wouldn't want you to get lost.'

'Look out for the maniac, then,' said Puggy.

Ducking under a low branch behind Maltravers Victoria could not help smiling.

'This used to be a rose walk,' Maltravers said, leading her along a narrow path knee-deep in grass and thistles. He reached the top of a little bank and stretched back to help her. Crouched against the incline her toe slipped and she fell to one knee, scrabbling for a foothold.

'I'm all right,' she said gaily but he was already leading her farther into the shrubbery. He was frowning, trying to match his memories against this overgrown profusion. She had to duck to avoid leafy branches whipping back into her face. Whenever he glanced back she tried to look composed. The showing of weakness was not the way to stimulate Julian, she had realised that only quite recently...

For several minutes Puggy sat against the tree-trunk staring at irregular segments of blue sky through many layers of foliage. Jock was still lying with his eyes closed.

The thickset, balding cameraman stood up, stretching his arms with a loud yawn. Jock did not move. Puggy took a few steps. When he looked back Jock was still motionless.

Strolling tentatively at first, occasionally standing on a log to peer through the dense greenery, Puggy made his way into the heart of the island, telling himself he was simply taking a stroll.

Yet at every step his eyes flicked from side to side and his ears strained to catch the sound of voices. His heart was thumping. Surely there was nothing between her and Julian? He could think of nothing else but Victoria, her arms, her hair, her voice, her beautiful shoulders and—no, she couldn't, not with *Julian*...

As soon as he felt the vibrations of Puggy's footsteps fading Jock Weir sat up and grabbed at Julian's hold-all, fingers probing down until they touched the smooth, solid weight of the whisky bottle.

'Would they *ever* bloody go?' he muttered.

He took the second mouthful more slowly, then screwed the cap back on the bottle and put it back in the bag.

'He'll never notice,' he said, doubtfully. Then he snorted. Why feel guilty about a drop of scotch?

His hand was reaching again for the bottle when he heard a sharp, cracking sound. Quickly he scrambled away from the hold-all, not looking round until he was lying in his original position. Nobody appeared.

It must have been a bird or a rabbit. He was sweating. The water far below looked very cool and he could imagine his hot, sticky body sinking gratefully beneath the sparkling surface. Through the woods came muffled echoes of peacock screams. His eye caught a flash of yellow.

A platoon of large wasps were buzzing over a half-eaten sandwich. He stood up. His throat was demanding another drink. As he stood over the hold-all he quickly scanned the bushes and ferns. He didn't think she would try to spy on him, but—

The black monk's cowl didn't move fast enough. Just for a second he saw it, then it was out of sight in the ferns. His face went red.

'I spy with my little eye a director all dressed up in drag,' he said. Another ten seconds and Julian would have seen him at the whisky bottle.

He sat down, trying to look like a man who wasn't screaming for a drink. He heard a movement in the ferns and thought he saw the black cowl again.

'You can come out now, you sneaky swine,' he called. Nothing happened. He stood up again, nonchalantly smoothing his silver-grey hair. 'Julian?'

* * *

'So—this is where you had your adolescent lustings,' Victoria said archly. They were at the bottom of a little hollow, a natural sun-trap formed by high banks on which grew massive hydrangeas and tall foxgloves.

'Beautiful little grotto, this was,' said Maltravers, shaking his head. His voice was distant.

'You and this serving-wench. I bet she thought you were a real catch. Did she have rosy cheeks and milk-white udders?'

'Nothing comes easier to us swinging sophisticates than the quick sneer, does it?'

'Oh. Sensitive, are we? Wasn't the reality as dreamy as the memory?'

'Give me a moment to work that out.'

'Simple enough. Did something go wrong—hang-ups are—'

'No hang-ups on my part,' he said brusquely. 'One of the other servants found out and informed Her Lady-ship. The girl got the sack. Quite an ordeal for a girl of that class, to go home to her parents in disgrace.'

'And what did they do to the gallant young Julian? The horsewhip? No, of course not, servant-girls are fair game for rich men's sons.'

'You know all the clichés, Victoria. As a matter of fact Lady Bennett was most understanding.'

'But not where the girl was concerned? Oh no.'

'The authentic voice of Women's Lib. Life isn't quite so simple.'

'Don't be coy.'

He bent down to pull a dandelion stalk. His first puff scattered half of the downy ball into the air between them. He had often wondered how it would sound.

'Quite an awe-inspiring person, Lady Bennett,' he said. 'I was terrified. You've got the wrong idea about the wealthy—our kind of wealthy anyway. My father belonged to the old school—a son, a dog, a horse, you

105

fed 'em well and if they played up you took the whip to 'em.'

He blew the rest of the seeds into the air and stared at the denuded stalk. Perhaps it would be *useful*, to tell someone else, after all these years.

'Lady Bennett said she ought to tell my father. I deserved punishment, as well as the girl. Would I rather have my punishment from her or my father?'

'How old was this Lady Bennett?' Victoria asked, looking amused.

'God knows, she seemed old to me, in her forties, something like that. A handsome woman, small but imposing. The girl—Thelma—had told me things about her but what does one know at fourteen? Anyway, I thought she would be fairly easy on me, my mother was always punishing me half-heartedly to save me from my father, I thought it would be the same sort of thing...'

'Do go on!'

'Mmm. Oh well. She obviously had a thing about young boys—doesn't sound much now, not in these enlightened times—' he pressed the lower end of the stalk on his palm, making a series of little circles—'she gave me a hearty thrashing on my bare backside, with a cane, no less. Then she came on all motherly and wanted to rub ointment on it and all that.' He crushed the milky stalk between his palms and threw it away. 'What do Women's Libbers say about the possibility of rape by a woman? By a much older woman—on a frightened boy?'

'You mean she actually—'

'Oh yeah. The whole bit. Randy old thing, she was.'

'So that was why you were so keen on coming here!'

'Did you expect me to put it in a memo? Anyhow, you don't even know if it's true or not.'

'You couldn't make a thing like that up.'

'Really? What am I doing in television, then?'

'Don't get aggressive with me now. I won't tell any-one else if you don't want me to.'

'Of course I don't want you to!'

'It wouldn't matter how trivial it was, anything personal makes you uneasy, Julian, I've noticed—'

'Yes, I'm emotionally frigid. I've been told. Is it any worse than your kind of frigidity?'

'Because I don't jump into bed with any man who fancies a quick bit on the side?'

'Or loves you.'

'Loves me? You mean Puggy? Jesus Christ, Julian, that isn't love, that's—I dunno what it is but it's ludicrous. Anyway, what makes you think you know anything about love?'

'I did, once.' He stared at her heavily. 'Getting turned on, that's the best we can expect these days, so why don't you—'

They both heard the sound of someone moving on the other side of the bank. Together they crouched down, his finger on his lips. Her thighs pressed heavily against her white trousers. They heard feet moving through grass, a few steps at a time. To whisper in her ear he had to put his face close enough for her red hair to brush his nose and cheeks.

'Wait here, don't make a sound.'

Stealthily, on all-fours, he moved up the little slope and tenderly, hardly breathing, parted the foxgloves. He turned to look back down at Victoria, motioning her to stay in the hollow.

Instead she crept up beside him. Their bodies were touching. He put his finger on her lips. His other hand rested on the bare skin where her cardigan was pulling up from her trousers. She peered through the stalks.

'Hullo, Puggy,' she drawled before he could stop her. 'Now it's your turn to hide.'

Maltravers got up quickly. For a moment he thought he was going to slap her. Puggy was blushing all over, even on his bald part.

'Oh, it's you,' he blurted. 'I was looking for a place to crap.'

Victoria sniggered.

They started back, Puggy in front, walking quickly. When he was ten yards ahead, not looking round, she grabbed Maltravers' arm and fell against him, laughing.

'Isn't he *ludicrous*? Doing his Peeping Tom act?'

He quickly freed his arm. In laughter her face was unmistakably cruel.

The figure in the cowl moved towards Jock Weir.

'Piss off, Julian,' he said, turning his back and scratching his neck. Then he heard voices.

When he looked round Maltravers and Victoria were appearing through the trees. He stared at them uncomprehendingly. When he looked at where the cowl had been he could see the ferns still shaking.

'Oh, it was Puggy,' he exclaimed. 'Getting quite playful in his old age.'

'He thought he would sneak up and catch us doing something naughty,' Victoria said sarcastically.

'He was here—a second ago.'

'Couldn't have been, we left him back in the woods attending to Nature's call,' said Maltravers.

'But—'

Puggy came down from the trees, whistling.

Weir looked at their faces but they were not having a game. He felt frightened. That cowl had been there. Or had it?

He shuddered.

'You all right, Jock?' Puggy asked.

'Yeah, just a bit hot.'

He couldn't tell them. He knew exactly what their

reaction would be: Jock's really been hitting it hard this time, booze has finally got to his brain, wonder how long he'll be able to hold onto the job.

Hallucinations! That was serious.

'Right then, Puggy and I will head over to the clay-pool,' said Maltravers. 'After that there's an old well that somebody brought stone by stone from Venice. One of you two will have to come with us.'

'Why?' asked Victoria.

'I want somebody to bring the cans of exposed film back up to this end of the island and hide them.'

'Why do you want to hide them?' she asked.

'Because if we get nabbed by the cops at the castle they'll confiscate any film we have on us, right?' He wasn't bothering to hide his impatience. 'If we hide the cans we can slip back for them later. It's a precaution, isn't it?'

'Good thinking,' she said, grudgingly. 'I'll come with you.'

'I'm coming, too,' Weir said hastily.

'No need for both of you trekking about in the jungle.'

'I'm not staying here by myself,' Weir said.

'In that case I'll stay,' said Victoria. 'With no Peeping Toms about I can get a proper tan.'

Puggy looked away, his face going a deep red.

She waited some minutes until she was sure they had not stopped behind the trees. She moved deeper into the tall ferns until she found a little open stretch of grass. She took off her cardigan and then her bra, exposing her heavy breasts to the sun. She lay on her back and stared up at the blue sky. She felt pleased with herself. But for Puggy blundering in on them like that Julian would have tried something. She wondered what she would have done. Two ducks flew over, wings working with mechanical regularity, necks straining forward, racing headlong. She remembered how ducks flew like that from the farm in Essex. Uncle Stan's farm. They made each flight seem vitally important but they only flew like that because they weren't very good at it.

She turned over on her stomach, resting her cheek on her forearm. A little red ant crawled among the gingery hairs on her wrist. Puggy looked a bit like Uncle Stan. What a revolting thought! Perhaps, when it happened, she might not have wanted to slide away from Julian. He was the only man she could think of who didn't disgust her. So cool and remote. Was that story true? Julian with his Lady Bennett and Victoria with her Uncle Stan? A certain neat geometry. What would it be like, with Julian? She blew the ant off her wrist and closed her eyes. She saw herself in the large, sunny house, glossy furniture, french windows, a sprinkler on a lawn, a long table set for lunch, the sparkle of long-stemmed glasses, a perfect baby in a white christening robe trimmed with lace. Yes Ma'am said the maid with the starched cap. Try as she could it was impossible to bring Julian into that sunny room. Unless, of course, he was the maid! . . .

She was sleeping, hidden among the ferns, while a few yards away the squat figure in the monk's robe peered down through the split trunk of a massive stone pine. The clearing was deserted. Black cloth trailed on grass as the dumpy, cowled figure hurried off into the woods. The woman must have gone with the others after all.

CHAPTER TWELVE

'Bahamas?' said Daniels into the phone.

'I've got a call booked to him at this very moment,' said Mr Bates, the London solicitor's chief clerk. 'He isn't in very good health, all this won't do him any good.'

Daniels finally put down the phone. That idea seemed to be a non-starter. Naturally Groves wanted to know whom he had been phoning. Daniels told him.

'A million pounds is a pretty good motive. However, the estate goes to an elderly gent in the Bahamas, Sir Godfrey's half-brother. He's seventy-four. Bed-ridden.'

'You think it hadn't occurred to me?' Groves said airily. 'It's an entailed estate, passes automatically to the next heir.'

'The heir might have been impatient.'

'Read a lot of trashy detective novels, do you?'

Daniels smiled. He was only too happy to let Groves indulge his taste for sarcasm, now that he'd decided to do it his own way.

'I went to see Sidney Marley yesterday,' he said casually.

'Who?'

'Marley, the man Llewellyn phoned about.'

Groves gave him a quick look.

'And?'

'I think he's telling the truth.'

Groves thought about that. Then he shrugged. He got up and leaned his gut against the window-sill, looking down at the neat lines of parked cars.

'What are you suggesting—the island's haunted? Spooks? Vampires? I told you not to waste time on that rubbish.'

When Groves was upset he had a habit of sucking air noisily through his front teeth. It was a mannerism that Daniels had come to loathe. He decided to bring everything into the open.

'You should know about wasting—' he began. The phone rang. He picked it up. 'Daniels,' he said. Groves was staring at him angrily. 'Yes!' he said. He started to scribble urgently. 'Tell them to wait there, we'll be down in ten minutes, don't touch anything.'

He put down the phone and got to his feet.

'You were saying?' Groves demanded.

'Somebody tried to steal a cabin-cruiser at the Old Town Yacht Club moorings over the weekend, broke into two of them—and there's a dinghy missing.'

'Old Town? We checked there yesterday. Why the hell didn't we know about it?'

'This chap didn't go out to his boat until this morning—'

'We're on our way!' said Groves. He looked triumphant. As he strode to the door Daniels lifted his jacket off the back of the chair.

'No, you stay here,' Groves said, 'something might crop up.' He disappeared into the big office. 'Right, then,' he was shouting, 'where's the fingerprint genius, get him back from the island, tell the launch to go straight to Old Town moorings—yes, Butler, two cars, three cars, all the men we've got, somebody along Shore Drive must have seen something, we'll do a house-to-house . . .'

Off he went in a bustle of shouts and hurrying constables. Daniels sat down at his desk. He swore. That lucky bastard! He would probably come back with the whole thing sewn up. The stolen dinghy was just what he had been waiting for.

The worst of it was, just enough had been said to let Groves know the score between them. He swore again.

Too angry with himself to think of anything else to do he picked up the wad of stapled foolscap sheets and began to read Lady Bennett's will in full. At least he would know the correct legal jargon when he came to dispose of his own fortune.

Puggy gave Jock the new can of exposed film. Jock seemed reluctant to leave them.

'Go on, then,' Maltravers said, 'toddle off back to Victoria and shove this can in with the others and then stash the bag up at the other end of the island, where those big pines are.'

'Isn't all this too cloak-and-daggerish for words? You aren't going to be caught and—'

'On your way, amigo.'

'It would only be trespassing, at the worst.'

'The police would hold onto the film,' said Puggy. 'It might take weeks to get it back—'

'During which time the island is thrown open and our chance of making a quick killing gone.' Maltravers patted Jock on the arm. 'This way one of us could sneak back at dead of night and rescue the vital celluloid and once again Mad Maltravers triumphs!'

He pointed dramatically.

'Oh well,' said Jock. They watched until he was out of sight.

'Typical product of our urbanised times,' said Maltravers. 'Thinks all birds are called sparrows and gets the jitters if he can't see neon lights. Did you smell the whisky?'

'Can't say I did.'

'Your solidarity is heart-warming. Let's get down to the castle.'

They crouched under a clump of rhododendron large enough to conceal a cottage. Puggy nudged Maltravers' arm. They watched two uniformed policemen walking slowly round the castle, stopping to examine a tree, one of them shaking a branch and then beating his chest with a Tarzan bellow. One of them went through the motions of bowling an invisible cricket ball. The other made an imaginary catch, whipped off invisible bails and threw an invisible ball into the air, arms wide as he shouted 'Howzat?'

'Can we get them on film?' Maltravers whispered excitedly.

'I'll have to move a bit to the left.'

The constables lit cigarettes. One of them stuck his cigarette in his ear and pranced about in goonish fashion. The other stuck his cigarette up his nostril. They were laughing as they walked towards the graveyard.

'Here,' said Puggy, taking his eye from the viewfinder, 'there's a grave been opened up.'

'Get it all!'

'The stone seems to be lying across it. What's that all about?'

'Film now, think later.'

The policemen suddenly decided to go round to the other side of the castle. Puggy tracked down the slope of tangled shrubbery, swivelling carefully on one knee, the zoom lens following a line that began at an ivy-strangled oak tree and went down the grassy slope to the walls of the castle and then along to the church and the graveyard, closing in on the clearly visible shape of the marble warrior. He held that in frame for ten seconds and then opened up the shot to take in the church tower, the castle and the yacht sails beyond.

'Okay?' said Maltravers.

Puggy was looking back up the slope.

'I thought I saw something moving up there, black—can't see it now, though.'

'Blackbird, maybe.'

'Bigger than that. Anyway, you've got two minutes thirteen left on this roll.'

'Let's see if those cops come back.'

They sat down, elbows on knees.

'Curious building,' Maltravers said. 'Exactly the right setting for a gory English-style murder.'

'Only this isn't a B picture and those guys were actually killed.'

'I wonder what he'll be like.'

'Who?'

'The folk-hero elect—the murderer.'

'What do you mean, hero?'

'Great people, us English, just as we're losing our affection for the last monster along comes another, stabbing eyes out, ripping throats, smashing heads—'

'Affection?'

'Hero-worship, then. Think of them, Christie, Crippen, Haigh, Joseph Smith tipping his brides into the bath. Heroes one and all.'

Puggy snorted.

'You never wanted to murder anyone? Oh, I forgot, daddy of them all, Jack the Ripper! Of course you've felt it, the—'

'Frequently. That's why we have laws and policemen and gaols.'

'And hangmen?'

Puggy thought about that for a moment.

'Ah!' he said knowingly, slapping Maltravers' arm, 'now they've stopped hanging these heroes of yours the fun's gone out of it, hasn't it? That last guy, the mass poisoner, he won't be one of the all-time greats, a life sentence isn't anything compared to the rope, is it?'

'You have brief moments of startling perception.'

'You know what I've always suspected about people like you—in this business, I mean? You've got all these advanced ideas about abolishing hanging and everything but deep down you're panting for the day when they'll let you film people actually being killed.'

'It's called the news, actually.'

'Be flippant if you like. I've seen it, mate, death, in all its revolting obscenity. You ever saw it you'd never talk about those ghouls like that.'

'Oh, I don't know.'

Jock was whistling loudly as he came back through the trees. Victoria was nowhere to be seen. He put the latest can of film into the hold-all. He saw Julian's bag but felt no urge to reach for the whisky. When you started seeing imaginary men in monks' cowls that was the time to get a grip on yourself.

'Victoria?'

There was no reply. She must be sunbathing in the undergrowth somewhere. He headed up through the trees. Midges swarmed above his head.

He found himself at the opening to a long, straight tunnel cut through a dark underworld of tightly packed rhododendron branches. He could see a semi-circle of light at the other end but hesitated. There seemed to be no other way round.

He entered the tunnel. A weak light filtered down through the overhead branches. Here and there at a break in the impenetrable walls he could see a little way into a dead, sunless world. Such was the silence that he might have been walking on some mysterious seabed.

'Phew,' he whistled when he came out into the sunlight. He lit a cigarette. While throwing away the match he seemed to catch a quick movement across the light at the other end of the tunnel. He looked again but there was nothing there. Then he remembered something he'd seen on television about careless picnickers starting forest fires.

He looked among some dandelions until he found the match. Naturally it was safely dead.

The high mound on which stood the tall pines was across to his left. Far below, stretching to the dark silhouette of a smaller island, the sun's reflection on the faintly tippled water was the shape of a huge dagger, the broad handle almost touching the tip of Peacock Island, a dazzling shimmer of golden light. He frowned.

Some twenty yards or so out from the stony shore below him an iron pole stuck out of the water. On top of it perched a large black bird, its wings motionlessly extended, its long neck curved as if preparing to strike.

It looked exactly like a vulture, frozen in the act of swooping down on a helpless victim. He thought of the murders—eyes torn out—a throat slashed and ripped. He shuddered.

He began to move quickly, crossing an exposed patch of rabbit-shorn grass. He saw another iron pole and another huge black bird in an identical position, wings fully extended, going nowhere. There were no boats on the vast waters of the harbour, no life of any description, just himself high on a hill and the two perching birds.

One of them swooped down off its isolated perch and set off across the harbour, flying in a dead straight line, only a few inches above the water, so low it merged with its own reflection, flying on such a precise course and height it seemed supernatural.

He made his way quickly towards the sacred mound. Feet pressing soundlessly on a thick layer of pine-needles, he walked among the tall, straight trunks. The sooner he ditched this bag and got back to the others the better. The hallucinations were becoming eerier every minute.

Where the rim of the mound fell sharply down a bushy slope to a little shingle beach he saw a thick out-crop of brambles.

'It's all games with Julian,' he muttered as he knelt down and started to lower the bag into the thorny creepers.

A faint rustle and a sense of movement behind him, vibrations, a swishing noise, all reached him at once. He had no time to look round. Something crashed onto his back.

He started to yell but his face was being pushed down into a springy bed of pine-needles and brown compost. He could not shake the weight off his back.

Needles jabbed softly into his eyes and nose and mouth...

CHAPTER THIRTEEN

'Well?' Groves strode into the small office. 'What are you looking so pleased about?'

Daniels knew how Groves must be feeling. Two cabin-cruisers had been broken into, certainly, but it had not taken the house-to-house teams long to find an elderly resident who had seen two Carter Street Secondary boys larking about with a dinghy on Saturday evening.

'He said he didn't think it was any of his business, the stupid old dotard,' Groves growled. 'The dinghy was only just round the corner on the other side of the old breakwater. Did I give that old fool a lecture about civic responsibility! People of that class—ratepayers! If they won't co-operate with us what chance do we have? Eh?'

'I got well used to public indifference in London.'

'Really? Has the old man been on? He'll be wanting to ask your old mates at the Yard for help on this one.'

'I haven't spoken to him.'

'So what've you been doing?'

'I've been reading Lady Bennett's will,' Daniels said casually.

Groves' phone rang. He listened briefly.

'Right away, sir,' he said. He put down the phone. 'The old man wants to hear a progress report. The station inspector wants to know if we're going to keep those four men out at the castle.'

He waited for Daniels' opinion. Daniels offered none. Groves picked up the phone and asked for the station inspector. Daniels listened patiently. They agreed to seal up the castle and put warning notices on all possible landing places. The four men could be brought back for normal duties. Groves put down the phone.

'Now for the old man,' he said, leaving the office. Daniels put in a call to the police at Lewes in Sussex. He spoke to the duty CID sergeant. He was sitting back in his chair when Groves returned, looking depressed.

'He'll decide tomorrow,' he said gloomily. 'If we don't make any more progress he'll make formal application for the assistance of a Murder Squad man. *That*'ll cost a few bob. Saturation detection, it's all these London big shots know. Finger-print every grown male in the county—bring in computers. Lot of balls.' He sniffed and then his face cheered a little. 'Still, I don't know where they'll start on that kind of operation. Not like as though we had a vague description of a car, or a piece of clothing with a convenient dry-cleaning label. I'm convinced it's a local. And somebody must know ... wife, mother, somebody. Here—this old gent in the Bahamas, the one who inherits, wonder if he'd put up a private reward? Ten thousand smackers buys a lot of co-operation...' His voice trailed off.

'As I said, I've been reading the will.'

'Makes you jealous, does it?'

'It's given me a little idea. You want me to stick with it for a while?'

'What the hell is it?'

'The will isn't as straightforward as I thought. The Honourable Goutylegs gets everything but there's a condition. He only gets her private money—that's apart from the entailed estate—provided—I'll read it—provided he makes due and ample provision for the care and well-being during his lifetime of Richard Cavendish Smith, resident at St Jude's Residential School, near Lewes, Sussex, such expenses not to be less than twenty thousand a year.'

'Who's this fellow, then?' Groves asked without much interest.

'That's just it, nobody seems to know.'

'What do you mean, *nobody*, the solicitors—'

'I've been onto them again. The partner who came down here to draw up her will in fifty-six is dead. All they know is that during his lifetime Richard Cavendish Smith is to be taken care of to the tune of twenty grand a year. He was obviously a minor at that time, there's two guardians listed, the headmaster of St Jude's and whoever is the senior partner of Kenworthy, Kenworthy, Frowd.'

'A schoolboy. Probably a poor cousin or something.'

'A schoolboy fourteen years ago.'

'You could give the school a ring. I'm looking forward to seeing how our high-powered genius from Scotland Yard proposes to tackle it. I can't think of anything we haven't done, can you?'

'I've already tried St Jude's,' Daniels went on calmly. 'No reply, holidays I suppose. Anyway, I've asked Lewes police to find out where the headmaster can be located.'

Groves shrugged.

'If it keeps you occupied.'

Half an hour later the call came from Lewes. The Reverend Thomas Thumbwood, headmaster and proprietor of St Jude's, had taken a small party of pupils on holiday to Eastbourne.

'Must be an adventurous establishment,' Daniels said to the Lewes CID man, 'he might at least have taken them to a different county. I thought they all went on Mediterranean cruises these days.'

'It's not so easy for this lot,' said the sergeant, 'it's a special school for abnormal kids—'

Daniels felt a jag of excitement in his stomach.

'What kind of abnormal?'

'Not mental—spastics and that sort of thing—quite a few of them in wheelchairs, poor little beggars.'

'It's no use looking in that direction for our killer, then,' Groves said, sarcastic as ever. 'I'm going out for a pint. I'll be in the back bar of the George if you come up with any more revelations.'

Daniels allowed himself the indulgence of a two-fingered salute behind Groves' back. He then asked directory enquiries to get him the number of the holiday house at which Mr Thumbwood was staying with his sad little party. It wasn't a lead but there was nothing else to do.

While waiting for the call he told Sergeant Butler to organise a cup of tea and two rounds of fried bacon on brown bread. Now that Groves had given up the struggle he could easily have gone home. But something was still nagging at him. It felt exactly as if he'd made a firm mental note of a birthday date and then forgotten whose birthday it was. Gould's helmet, for instance, the dogs would have sniffed it out if it had only fallen into some long grass. And there was something else—was it that first time he went through the castle? Something he had seen, something not quite right...

A woman answered the phone. He asked for Mr Thumbwood. She gave him the helpful information that Mr Thumbwood had gone out with his boys on his favourite recreational pursuit of taking brass-rubbings from old gravestones. The charity which owned the holiday home had a converted mini-bus for the handicapped children. In which Sussex burial ground he was indulging his hobby she did not know. She promised to get Mr Thumbwood to phone Mundham police station as soon as he returned.

Daniels got up and looked out of the window. There was one small spot, above a rooftop lower than the rest, where you could see the treetops on Peacock Island. He shut his eyes and tried to remember every step he had taken through the castle.

'Damn and blast and shit!'

Victoria Dryden-Chambers awoke to find her naked breasts and shoulders on fire. She had been asleep for ages. Now she was burned all over and her skin would peel and she would look *awful*.

'Damn, damn, damn!'

She fastened her bra, wincing as the half-cups rubbed on tender skin. She eased her arms into the sleeves of the light blue cardigan. Eyes muzzy and head slightly giddy she got to her feet. She heard the scream of a peacock. Her watch said it was half past four. Already her skin was going hot and cold in turns. She brushed through the ferns, tears of anger coming to her eyes.

When Maltravers and Puggy returned to the little encampment they saw immediately that she had been crying.

'What's up then, sweetness?' Maltravers asked, putting his arm round her shoulders. She hissed with pain, jumping free of his touch.

122

'Where's Jock?' asked Puggy.

She muttered something.

'What did you say?'

'I was sunbathing over there, I fell asleep and now I'm sunburned all over and I don't know where Jock is and I don't bloody well care!'

'Oh.'

'I'm shattered,' said Maltravers, flopping down on a spread-out nylon parka. 'The heat! The mosquito bites! I notice they don't bite you, Puggy, too bloody tough for them. I think I'll risk everything and have a cigarette. You got one to spare, Victoria?'

She was pulling a comb through her red hair. She kicked her folded leather coat a little way towards him. It would have been less effort to crawl a yard on his hands and his knees but he stood up. Accidental or not, he wasn't going to be caught *crawling* before her.

'Pity we don't have the boat right now,' he said, 'we could whip round the island and do the front of the castle. Shouldn't take long in the morning.'

'You've got enough, haven't you?' she said, irritably. 'I want to get back to London, even if we have to drive all night. I hate this place.'

Maltravers looked at Puggy.

'We need some establishing shots to show this *is* an island, sweetness. No point in spoiling the ship for whatever that old-fashioned coin was.'

The silence was embarrassing.

A few yards away in the ferns the cowled figure strained to hear what they were saying now. Through green fronds the deeply shaded eyes caught a glimpse of Victoria's red hair. The sound of The Keeper's breathing became much more pronounced.

'Thank God for a breeze,' said Victoria as they came out of the clammy stillness of the woods and found they were looking across an open space of heather and gorse between them and the sacred mound.

'We have seen Paradise and it's decidedly sticky,' said Maltravers.

'I can't see Jock.' Puggy was shading his eyes with his hands, staring at the almost geometrically regular clump of pines. They walked between thickets of gorse. The loaf-shaped silhouette of one of the harbour's smaller islands was dark against the western sun. A black cormorant was drying its extended wings on a pole after a fishing expedition. It flew off across the dazzle of reflected sunlight, heading for the darkening green of the harbour's farthest recesses. Like a spirit of the dead, Maltravers thought, flying so low the dark shadow on the water seemed to be another, perfectly shaped bird.

'There's a house on that island over there,' he said. 'It was up for sale a few years back, a mere sixty-five thousand.'

'A give-away,' said Puggy. 'I wonder what the inflation price is.'

'You couldn't *pay* me that much to live on a stinking place like this,' said Victoria. 'Quite apart from being fried I'm covered with bites.'

And you're also blushing, Maltravers thought. Imagine forgetting all about the establishing shots! That wasn't how you built up a slick professional image. As he looked round he felt strangely sad. It was easy to see why primitive people would imbue this spot with magic. The sun was beginning to sink over the vast amphitheatre of the harbour, the changing angle of its rays making dramatic contrasts between the hazy contours of the green and gold hills and the shining water.

'You know now why they don't have women presidents and prime ministers,' Puggy suddenly said, giving Victoria a cheery nudge.

'What do you mean?' she demanded.

'Well,' his smile becoming less certain, 'I mean, a few midge bites and we might be in the middle of the nuclear holocaust.'

'Because I forgot the establishing shots?' She was angry and Maltravers could see that Puggy had no idea how to smooth it over.

'I was only joking,' he stammered.

'Up yours,' she snapped.

'And so we say goodbye to Murder Isle as the sun sinks in the golden west,' drawled Maltravers in a mock travelogue voice.

They climbed onto the springy surface of the mound.

'Ehm, Victoria, I'll get some good panoramic stuff here, eh?' said Puggy.

'You're the bloody expert,' she said, glaring at him viciously.

'I only—'

Much as he enjoyed spectating at a good snarling-match Maltravers decided to stay clear of the crossfire. He walked to the very edge of the mound. Behind him Puggy's voice was low and pleading, Victoria's a series of staccato monosyllables. Maltravers looked down to the beach and the path they had come up that morning in the half light.

'Jock?' he called.

'I don't bloody care,' Victoria said curtly.

It was then he saw the hold-all, sticking out of a patch of heather, about half way down the steep slope.

'Come here, you two,' he called.

They looked down.

'Yes, that's the bag with the cans of film,' said Victoria. 'The careless idiot—where the hell is he?'

'I'll go down and get it,' said Puggy.

As he slid over the edge he looked up at her tear-streaked face. Her eyes met his. She stared right through him. What the hell had prompted him to try and make a joke like that?

Thick clumps of white heather gave his hands something to grasp as his feet probed down for each new foothold. He saw Julian's fair head moving down the path. He turned sideways, looking down past his stomach as his toe searched for something solid. Extending his right foot he managed to push the bag over and hook his toe into the handle strap. He began to lift.

He reached down and grabbed it with his right hand. There were no cans in it. He slithered down as far as the heather but if they had fallen out they must have gone all the way to the bottom.

'It drops away very sharply there, be careful,' Maltravers shouted across the little bushy gorge.

'Can you see any cans?' he called back.

'No.'

He poked his foot into the heather and then began to pull himself back up the slope. Victoria made no move to help him struggle back onto the flat surface. When he stood up they were facing each other.

'Look, I'm sorry, I didn't mean anything,' he said, 'don't get all sore about nothing, Victoria. You know I wouldn't—'

'Julian's down there looking,' she said coldly.

'That bugger Weir, if he's lost those cans—'

He went off down the path. At the bottom of the gorge he heard Maltravers moving about in the thick bushes that grew down the stony bed of what had once been an ornamental stream.

'Jock?' they both called. They went down to the shore and found themselves walking on a beach made of broken drainage pipes, a crunching expanse of dark brown shards, jagged edges worn smooth by the tides of a hundred years.

Maltravers climbed on the timbers of the old clayworks jetty and walked out a few yards. Before him a line of black piles stuck out of the water like a row of rotten teeth. Looking down he saw shoals of small fish, thousands of them now churning the surface of the water, now darting deep in unison, silver belly-scales cascading through opaquely green water.

'Brit,' said Puggy coming up behind him, 'just tiddlers.'

'He couldn't be down there—no.'

'The bastard deserves to be. The film's gone—every single bloody can.'

'We'd better—'

They both heard Victoria's shout. Looking up they saw her waving urgently over the edge of the sacred mound. They began to run.

She met them at the top of the path, her face agitated.

'I saw him! He was wearing that stupid monk's robe. He was down in those bushes!'

They looked where she was pointing. They saw nothing.

'He must be drunk!' Puggy cupped his hands and shouted, 'Come here, you bloody idiot!'

'He's only larking about,' said Maltravers. 'Get your magazine loaded, Puggy, we can get some good stuff here.'

Puggy got the black loading bag out of a hold-all. He took the magazine off the camera, placing it in the bag with a can of new stock. His hands moved carefully in the bag as he opened the can of film and felt for the magazine sprockets.

'He's not drunk on this one,' Maltravers said, holding up the whisky bottle. Rummaging in the same hold-all he found the last of the sandwiches.

'Plastic cheese in rapidly drying white bread,' he said, squatting down against a pine trunk. 'No wonder all the ploughmen stopped having lunch.'

'Is that all you're going to do?' Victoria demanded.

'You think I should race down there and gallop through the woods bellowing like Tarzan? If he *has* mucked the film up I shall personally strangle him for your personal delectation—'

'For Christ's sake, he's probably ruined a whole day's filming and all you can do is eat a sandwich!'

'Why don't you have a cup of tea—or a drop of scotch? You don't want to prove Puggy was right about—'

'You give me any of that prime minister bullshit, I'll—'

Maltravers smiled easily.

'Ah, woman of infinite moods and variations. On balance, Victoria, I think you get to me most when you're screaming mad, yes, it suits you, the colouring, the—'

She kicked a spray of pine needles into his face. He blinked and smiled again. He looked at the remains of the sandwich. He shrugged and threw it over his shoulder.

'I can understand how you feel,' he said. 'It's getting people to follow simple instructions. That's why great generals are so rare, they have the knack of making huge masses of bird-brains turn up where and when they are wanted.'

'That's why we guardsmen are the élite,' said Puggy, hands still in the bag.

Victoria glared at them in turn, hardly believing that they could talk like this. She wanted to scream.

'Victoria doesn't appreciate what the Guards mean, old boy, it's all the boring old army to her. Now, if you'd seen me in RAF blue, darling—'

'A well-tailored shambles, that's your air force,' said Puggy. Without changing his tone he said: 'You see where he is now—those bushes to your right—don't look!'

But Victoria turned immediately. The black cowled figure disappeared.

'He'll come back in a minute or two, don't worry,' said Maltravers. 'Next time we say don't look, Victoria, *don't* look.'

'You could see him all the time? I didn't realise— I'm sorry, I—'

'Never mind. We fighting chaps learned to communicate by telepathy.'

He gave her his most patronising wink. One thing about Victoria, she had enough intelligence to know when she was losing. He wondered if she was going to cry again. Puggy brought the loaded magazine out of the black bag and started to fit the distinctive, twin-wheeled shape onto the camera. Victoria searched in a hold-all for her handbag and walked off a few yards among the pine trunks, holding a compact mirror before her face.

'I'm going to smash Jock's face in,' Puggy said angrily.

'My vote's for castration,' said Maltravers, 'but keep it cool, I think our Victoria is going through a very rough patch.'

'And I think you're such a bastard you're enjoying the sight of her having a rough time.'

'It wasn't me who started all that women and nuclear button nonsense.'

'I could have kicked myself, it just came out!'

They both heard her shouting something across the mound.

'What's got her this time?' Maltravers said. 'Go on then, run over there, man, supply a strong shoulder. Perhaps you can save her from a sex-mad rabbit and win back her undying love.'

'You're a shit, you know that?'

'I always have.'

Puggy put down the camera and walked across the mound. Victoria was staring down at a spot where the pine needles had been disturbed.

'What is it?' Puggy asked, feeling so sorry for her he could have wrapped his arms round her there and then and cradled her against his chest.

'Look,' she hissed. 'Look at that!'

Puggy looked. It wasn't just the scrapings of a rabbit. The needles and soft brown earth had been pushed together into a long, narrow mound. At one end, sticking straight up, was a feather. He pulled it out. It was about five feet long, from the tail of a peacock.

'Go back over there beside Julian,' he said.

'What do you—'

'I said go over there!'

She went, looking back over her shoulder, stumbling slightly.

Puggy walked round the mound. His stomach was already turning.

'What is it?' Maltravers called.

He scraped at one end of the heap with his toe. Something solid touched his foot. He dragged more earth and needles clear with the sole of his shoe.

'Come on, what is it?' Maltravers shouted.

'It's a shoe,' Puggy said, disbelievingly. He reached down and touched it with outstretched fingertips. 'It's Jock's shoe!'

'What game is he playing now, that drunken bum? Give me his bloody shoe. I'm going to ram it down his throat.'

Puggy hesitated, his mouth opened, his stomach knotted with tension. He forced himself to take a grip of the protruding toecap. When he spoke his face was almost hysterical.

'He's still wearing it!'

CHAPTER FOURTEEN

Nobody spoke. From the water far below they heard a voice booming through a megaphone.

Puggy found a short twig. He started scraping into the soft loam of pine needles round the dirty suède toe-cap. He uncovered an inch or so of grey nylon sock. Then an inch of bare leg.

'Give me a hand, Julian,' he shouted.

Maltravers got slowly to his feet.

'Hurry up, he might still be alive!'

Maltravers swallowed hard. He forced himself to approach.

'Pull this way,' Puggy said, hands feeling in the rich brown dirt to get hold of the familiarly shabby sports jacket.

They dragged Jock's body free from its covering of needles and soil. Along with it came the cans of film. It looked as if they had been lying on his chest and stomach. His face was hidden under a mask of brown earth. Puggy knelt down and blew at the dirt.

There was no need to feel for the pulse. Lightly flecked with specks of soil, Jock's bulging eyeballs were glazed and sightless.

So tight that it was hidden in places by skin, the cord of the monk's habit was knotted at the back of his neck.

Victoria fell to her knees, moaning hysterically. From the dense heart of the island came the screams of the peacocks.

A few yards away, only one dark shadow among many

in the gloom under a weeping willow, The Keeper watched the red-haired woman. He waited to see which of them would run for help. Once they separated they would be no trouble.

Then he could get hold of the red-haired woman.

'Well, thank you very much, Mr Thumbwood,' said Daniels. He put down the phone.

Groves was speaking to Brigadier Wooldridge of Goat Island. The Brigadier resented heartily the insinuation that an intruder might be hiding on his private domain. Didn't he have trip-wires (attached, it was rumoured, to strategically placed shotguns loaded with rock salt), every known form of anti-burglar device *and* half a dozen enthusiastic bull-mastiffs? How, indeed, could any skulking criminal be hiding on his picturesque little death-trap?

'He said he'll be happy to lend us the mastiffs,' Groves said, putting down the phone. ' "Me dogs will rip the swine to pieces." '

Daniels smiled. He picked up his own phone again.

'I want you to get me the number of a sanatorium in Berkshire,' he said to the switchboard policewoman. 'It's called Willow Grange, it's in the Maidenhead area.'

'Well?' Groves demanded.

'A bit tired, that's all.'

'Don't be bloody funny! What did the reverend gentleman have to tell you?'

'Well, the boy isn't there now, of course. Lady Bennett told Thumbwood that she was Richard Cavendish Smith's godmother. His parents were killed in an air crash. She sent him to this St Jude's place after he'd been at another establishment in Switzerland. He's achondroplastic.'

'Is that bad?'

'It's a bone disease. Prevents growth. His legs are

deformed—very short. Mr Thumbwood had to ask Lady Bennett to take him away from St Jude's.'

'Christ, this is like dragging teeth. What did he do? And what's got into you?'

'Oh, boyish pranks. Strongly suspected of chucking the matron's cat into the boiler-room furnace. He also had something to do with a kitchen-maid drowning herself in the laundry-room copper. After he'd gone the other boys said he'd been terrorising her. They were all scared of him. Anyway, Lady Bennett had him put in a private institution, Thumbwood says he was obviously in need of psychiatric treatment.'

'He can afford the best now, then.'

'I'll have a word with this sanatorium, just to check.'

'Sounds like one of these new jokes. First the good news, you're rich. Now the bad news—you're insane.'

Neither of them smiled.

'We're going to have to look hard at these bloody alibis again,' Groves said, trying to sound brisk. 'Somebody's covering up for our man. I think we'll have to get a list of every bloody man who's ever taken a boat across this bloody harbour.'

'Always taking it for granted that it is a local,' said Daniels.

'Well, what the bloody hell else could he be?' Groves was near to exploding. Daniels looked at him impassively. 'Don't you sit there looking bloody quizzical! Doesn't it mean anything to you, falling on our faces? Having to get a London big shot in? I'll tell you something about you, Victor, you're a—'

Daniels' phone rang. He did not pick it up. He went on looking at Groves.

'Answer the bloody thing!'

It was the switchboard policewoman. Willow Grange Sanatorium had closed down in nineteen-sixty-seven. The place had been turned into a high-priced health farm. Nobody there knew the whereabouts of the sanatorium people.

'You might have known,' said Groves. 'Just one little break, that's all we need in this—'

Suddenly he shoved at his desk with both hands. The legs shuddered on linoleum.

'I'll be at home if anyone wants me,' he said bitterly, slamming the door open.

Daniels went to the window. In a minute or so Groves appeared in the car-park, walking heavily to his Cortina, two reporters trying to keep up with him. The car accelerated into the road. The two reporters stood in the middle of the car-park. Police baffled, tomorrow's headline.

Did it matter? At this moment some drunken, moronic couple might be beating a baby to death in those terraced slums by the gasworks. Would that bring reporters and television crews all the way from London? If Greeno and Gould had been killed in a car crash would anybody have shown interest?

It wasn't death that mattered, only the sideshow. The entertainment. Why was Groves near to blowing up? Why was he himself becoming all crafty and devious?

To see justice done? Out of genuine anguish over Gould's death?

Ego. That's what made detectives tick. Ego and obsessional curiosity. A craving for power as well. But mostly ego.

And nobody knew better than he where it all led to. It was almost six o'clock.

He presumed Groves wanted him to re-examine the suspects' alibis. He put his hand on the phone, to ask Butler for the files. He could work his way steadily through the reports for an hour or two. Maybe something would strike him. Probably not. The Chief would be asking for a Murder Squad man tomorrow. Let him see if he could work miracles.

As he put the phone to his ear he saw the heavy legal paper of Lady Bennett's will. That was one loose end he could clear up.

He asked the girl to get him the duty officer at Berkshire CID. They might know something about Willow Grange Sanatorium. This poor deformed bastard ought to be told that he was rich.

Puggy cradled Victoria's head in his elbow.

'Take a sip of this,' he said, holding the whisky bottle to her lips.

'He was murdered!' she gasped.

'That's it, just a sip.'

Maltravers stood over them, his face expressionless.

'That must have been the murderer—in the monk's robe,' he said.

'Shut up, Julian,' Puggy snapped. 'Come on, Victoria, you'll have to get on your feet.' As he helped her up he looked at Maltravers: 'We must get those cops at the castle.'

'Hang on a minute.'

Puggy could hardly believe it. Julian was picking up the cans of film and shoving them into a hold-all!

'For God's sake—Jock's been murdered!'

'Losing all this footage isn't going to resurrect him, is it?'

Victoria sobbed against Puggy's chest, her hair hiding her face.

They started through the pine trunks, not looking back at the lifeless figure partially covered by a blue nylon parka.

As they came into the dense heart of the island they took care to stay close to each other, eyes nervously scanning each bank of shrubbery, each turn and opening, breathing quickly in relief as they passed a massive tree-trunk, only to find another ahead of them.

They passed the grotto and skirted the gorse clearing of Pheasant Park. They came to a clump of bamboo and then circled the steep sides of the clay-pool, its blue waters so clear they could see every bump and hollow on the moonlike bottom.

Puggy reached back to help Victoria onto a slippery bank of coarse grass. Just for a second, looking back across the water, he caught sight of a movement.

'What is it?' Victoria demanded shrilly, slipping to her knees as she stared over her shoulder.

'Just a bird, a peacock probably. Let's hurry, it's getting dark in this bloody forest.'

They had gone only a few yards past the pool when they heard the voice. A young voice, a mischievous voice.

'See how they run,' it chanted.

Victoria's hands clamped on Puggy's arm. None of them moved.

'Catch me if you can,' came the voice again. A young man's voice.

'He's over there, behind that tree,' Maltravers hissed. 'The elder with the berries—you go that way, Puggy, I'll—'

Puggy grabbed his lapels.

'He *wants* us to split up, Julian, for God's sake keep going.'

The Keeper watched them hurrying clumsily down the slope. The blue of peacock feathers glinted momentarily in a patch of dying sunlight as he followed.

The red hair made him hot and excited in a way he had not felt for ages and ages and ages.

'Who killed your friend, then?' he chanted. 'Who killed your silly friend?'

'I only wish I'd thought to get in touch with you myself when I read the newspapers,' said Doctor Le

Quex. 'I'll start looking for my file on the boy straight away.'

'Much obliged,' said Daniels. He put down the phone. He picked it up again immediately. Alf was going to get his lucky break after all.

'The Chief Constable is on the line, sir,' said the switchboard girl before he could ask for Groves' home number.

Daniels hesitated a moment, a very short moment.

'Superintendent Groves has gone home, sir,' he said. 'However, something interesting has come up—right, sir, I'll come straight over.'

As he was leaving the small office he looked at Groves' empty chair.

'Sorry about this, old chap,' he said.

The old path took them on a gradual slope down to a disintegrating brick shed. Against the wall of what had been stables for ponies used in the old clay-diggings they saw a row of caged runs.

Grass and nettles grew high behind thin iron bars. Puggy, striding along beside Victoria, hand under her elbow, saw it first.

In one of the tall kennel-cages was a skeleton, white bones resting hard against rusty iron rails. Quickly he increased his step to block Victoria's view.

Then he realised it was the skeleton of a dog, the flat skull resting against the bars at a weirdly animated angle, a leather collar still round the neckbone, a chain hanging from the collar.

Maltravers saw what Puggy was staring at. That would have been a *great* shot, he thought. He looked at Puggy's anxious face. Shouldn't he feel guilty—thinking of shots while Weir lay back there with his eyes bulging out of his face?

In all honesty he had to admit it to himself. He felt

nothing. He wondered why.

The path dropped sharply to the left. They came down onto the tree-covered walk that ran beside the Roman bath.

When they looked back the light was too gloomy to tell if they were still being followed. They had not heard the voice again. Their foreheads glistened with sweat. Puggy was trying to force them into a run but Victoria had developed a slight limp.

Then they saw the church tower.

Victoria gasped, trying to slow down. Puggy kept a firm grip of her elbow.

As they came out onto the grassy slope behind the castle they started to shout.

'They must be round the front,' said Puggy.

There was no sun at the other side of the castle, its grey walls bleak and silent in its own premature dusk.

'Where are you?' Puggy shouted.

Victoria flopped down wearily on the little wall that ran across the castle forecourt.

'They must be inside,' said Maltravers, walking across mossy flagstones to the iron-studded door.

He banged the big black knocker three times. Hearing only its echo he tried to turn the handle. The door did not open.

It was then he saw the new metal flanges and the heavy padlock.

'They've sealed it,' he said.

'They couldn't just have gone—they must be on the quay.'

Puggy started to run towards the gap in the cottages. Victoria dropped her head, covering her face with her palms.

Her legs were aching. Her breathing was shallow and painful. For a moment she felt giddy.

She was too exhausted to be surprised when Julian

put his hand on her shoulder. He looked sad.

'When they start asking we'll tell them I was in full charge of this little expedition,' he said, quietly. She didn't understand. 'I'm better suited for notoriety,' he said. She watched him walk towards the cottages, still carrying the bag with the film. What did he mean? She groaned with relief as she eased off her shoes and let her bare feet touch cool moss.

When the suffocating blackness descended on her she knew immediately that it was Puggy's magazine-loading bag. She felt the soft cloth against her cheeks.

What a silly time to play jokes, she thought.

Then she felt the cord tightening around her neck . . .

Maltravers met Puggy on the quay.

'They're not here,' Puggy said grimly. 'They've gone!'

'That's marvellous.'

'If we shout loud enough they'll hear us on those yachts, noise travels better over water, doesn't it?'

'They're farther than they look.'

'We'll start a fire! It'll stand out a mile in this light.'

'What can we burn?'

'Our clothes, anything,' said Puggy. 'Victoria's got matches.'

As he started back he realised that the angle of the path between the cottages put the castle from out of sight from the quay.

'Victoria,' he was shouting as he started to run. 'You got your matches, Victoria?' he shouted, coming out onto the castle forecourt. 'We want to start a—'

Victoria was not there. Beside the little wall lay her shoes, one on its side.

'Victoria?'

He raced to one end of the castle, then the other.

'What's wrong?' called Maltravers, appearing between the cottages.

'She's not here!'

They ran together, up the side of the castle, round the grassy slope at the rear, shouting her name, panting heavily.

When they came back to the front of the castle her shoes were still lying there.

CHAPTER FIFTEEN

'Why did Superintendent Groves go home?' asked the Chief Constable.

'He hasn't had much sleep, sir, he's pretty well exhausted. I think he ought to know about this.'

'Tell me and we'll see if it's worth dragging him back.'

'Well, sir, he's bound to think—'

'Is it urgent?'

'Half an hour won't make any difference, sir. I'd rather phone him.'

'Okay.' The Chief watched Daniels picking up the white phone. 'Keen on protocol, are you, Daniels?' he asked.

Daniels held the phone to his ear.

'It is his case, sir.'

It was working out very well, he thought. Of course the very fact that he was here meant he was going behind Alf's back but not in any way Alf could complain about.

Bertie Groves answered the phone. Her name was Alberta but everyone called her Bertie, including Alf. She had short hair and ran a riding school. They had no children.

'He's parking the car now,' she said. 'Is it urgent?'

'Yes.'

'Naturally—always is when he just happens to get an evening to himself. Isn't it something you can cope with?'

'I'm speaking from the Chief Constable's office.'

'Oh.'

Alf came to the phone.

'I'm in the Chief Constable's office,' said Daniels. 'Something's come up.'

'Oh yes? Just happened to turn up—in the thirty-five minutes it took me to drive home? You think I'm stupid, Victor?'

'I think you ought to come back—'

'Couldn't wait to scurry round to his office, could you? I don't care how this case goes, I'm going to—'

'I found out about Richard Cavendish Smith,' Daniels said. 'I think he's our man.'

'What—this bloody dwarf of yours? I bet the Chief is impressed.'

'You want to speak to him?'

'You tricky bastard.'

Groves rang off.

'I think he's coming, sir,' Daniels said.

'*Think?*'

'Wasn't a good line, he sounded excited.'

The Chief Constable smiled.

'Get on well with Alf, do you?' He didn't wait for an answer. 'It took me some time to find his wave-length, I remember when I was first appointed, back in fifty-eight, Alf was a sergeant then, I'd only been in this office a day and...'

Daniels was looking at the firm mouth under the stiff little moustache. Nineteen-fifty-eight? The Chief went on talking. *Nineteen-fifty-eight?*

And then he remembered what had been nagging at him. A locked cupboard in the old kitchen, double-doors swinging on hinges that didn't squeak, the only hinges in the castle that didn't squeak or weren't hanging off. And cans—piled all the way to the top.

Nineteen-fifty-eight!

He looked at the clock. Alf would be here in twenty minutes. I've got it, he thought, his breathing getting a little faster. I've done it!

'...need to make the point that all of this is absolutely confidential, between you and me?' the Chief Constable was saying.

'Of course, sir,' Daniels said, not having listened to a word of it.

He looked at the clock. Come on, Alf, I want you to hear this, he said to himself.

He let the Chief Constable waffle on. There was no hurry. After all these years a few minutes wouldn't make much difference...

They hammered frantically on the doors of empty cottages. They dashed up the grassy slope at the rear of the castle, panting heavily, shouting her name, climbing higher into the heart of the island, crashing through faintly gleaming blossoms, tearing their clothes on thorns, their cries sending panic through unseen rows of roosting birds.

They got as far as the blue pool before Maltravers stopped.

'This is stupid,' he said, 'we have to get help.'

'VICTORIA! VICTORIA!'

Puggy's shouts echoed across the still water. They listened but heard only the outraged chimes of a pair of nesting blackbirds.

'He can't have taken her far,' Puggy said desperately, 'we've got to keep looking.'

'It's impossible in this light.'

Maltravers watched Puggy running round the pool, shouting her name into the trees.

She was almost certainly dead but Puggy wouldn't admit it. The strange thing was—he felt nothing. Why wasn't he going mad, like Puggy? He didn't feel that it was even happening, not in reality. There had been a flicker, with Victoria, just for a moment, but that was all. Only the same emptiness inside him. To think I laughed at you, Puggy. What is it like—to *feel* things?

When they came back to the castle they were both hurrying, hoping she would be standing there. Her shoes still lay beside the little wall. The sky overhead was a rich purple but down here it was almost dark. From the brightly-lit decks of large cruisers came the strains of music. They could see people moving against cabin lights.

Standing at the very edge of the quay they began to empty out their pockets. Puggy made a little pile of crushed envelopes, club cards, all the odds and ends men carried. He knelt over the crumpled papers.

They realised it instantaneously.

'Oh no!' Puggy's shoulders fell.

'So what do we do now?'

'I don't know ... Jesus Christ ... just a minute—Jock had matches!' Puggy scrambled to his feet. 'It won't take long.'

'In the dark? All the way up this bloody island again?' Maltravers shook his head. 'I'd rather take a chance and swim for it.'

He said this without thinking. It was just taken for granted that nobody risked swimming near Monks Sweep when the tide was turning. But Puggy was grabbing his arm.

'That's it,' he was saying, 'you can swim to those cruisers! I'd do it but I can't swim a stroke.'

Puggy didn't know about the currents. Maltravers looked out across the black water.

'No,' he said, shaking his head, 'leaving you here on your own—it's just what that maniac wants.'

Puggy snorted, gripping his arm even tighter.

'Jesus Christ, Julian, I'm the old Guardsman, remember, he comes near me I'll break his bloody neck for him! Don't worry about me, for Christ's sake!'

In the face of that what else was there to do?

Maltravers dropped his suède jacket on the quay and dragged his white sweater over his head. He took off his suède boots and white socks. When he hesitated Puggy immediately exclaimed:

'Don't worry about me, Julian, I'm telling you, I'll be okay. Just get help.'

'It's a nice night for a swim,' Maltravers said.

He dived in cleanly, with only a slight splash. His fair hair and white underwear formed a ghostly streak under the dark water. When he surfaced he shook his eyes clear.

'Good luck,' Puggy shouted down from the edge of the quay.

Maltravers sank his face into the water and with strong overarm strokes set off for the hulls of the brightly-lit cruisers.

Puggy picked up his jacket and turned back along the quay. Against the fiery red of the western sky the castle looked like a cardboard cut-out, a two-dimensional silhouette. He began to hurry. With Julian safely out of the way he could start looking for Victoria in earnest He *would* break the bastard's neck, too bloody right.

He didn't really blame Julian for being scared to go back into the island's woods.

Groves' face was set hard.

Daniels found no difficulty in suppressing an early

twinge of embarrassment. They were policemen, weren't they, not jealous actresses? The time for games had stopped.

Besides, he was enjoying himself.

'Berkshire CID put me onto the former medical superintendent of the sanatorium,' he was saying. 'Doctor Le Quex is his name, he remembers Richard Cavendish Smith well. He's deformed, it's a type of dwarfism known as achondroplasia, it stopped his legs from growing—but he isn't a cripple, he was mobile enough to get through the sanatorium's security and that included an eight-foot fence.'

'So where is he now, this *dwarf*?' Groves said icily.

'That's the point. He skipped from this sanatorium almost as soon as he arrived from St Jude's. In nineteen-fifty-eight. He was thirteen then.'

Groves looked at the Chief Constable but said nothing.

'Lady Bennett was told he'd gone the next morning. Two days later she wrote to say she'd found a place that suited the boy better. Le Quex wrote to her several times, he wanted to pass on his notes to the doctor who'd taken over the boy's case. She never replied. Le Quex didn't have him very long but his early diagnosis was that Smith was a potential psychopath with every sign of incipient schizophrenia.'

'She must have kept the correspondence with the new place she found for him,' said Groves. 'We'll have another dig through her papers. Have we got a description?'

'As a boy, yes. He was blond, quite good-looking according to Le Quex. Apart from his legs, that is.'

'Interesting,' said Groves, looking at the Chief Constable. He didn't need to say it. Was *this* what Daniel was so excited about? The Chief Constable looked a Daniels.

'I think he's our man,' Daniels said.

Groves was always at his most mocking when his face showed no expression at all.

'I've heard it called clutching at straws,' he said, looking at the ceiling.

'Le Quex has a copy of the boy's birth certificate.' Daniels went on calmly. 'The mother is down as Margot Cavendish. Father unknown. It's an Irish Republic certificate—he was born in a private nursing home in Dublin—'

'So he's an Irish bastard,' said Groves, sounding a lot cheerier. 'We'll need more than that.'

'Lady Bennett's maiden name was Margot Cavendish,' said Daniels, looking at his notes.

'I don't believe it!' Groves snorted. 'He was thirteen in nineteen-fifty-eight? And she was seventy-one this year? That means she would have been—ehm—'

'Forty-six,' said the Chief.

'Exactly, sir. Her first child? Nonsense.'

'I asked Barham,' said Daniels. 'It's fairly common for women to have first children at that age.'

'Nobody ever heard of her having a son. Nobody ever saw a boy on the island. I've lived here all my life, you know.'

'According to gossip she was fairly promiscuous—'

'I know all the gossip!' Groves was being challenged on his own ground and he didn't like it. What the hell did Daniels know about Mundham? 'You hear that about any rich widow. Anyway, it doesn't matter whose bastard he was—'

'I think it does,' said Daniels, turning over the pages of his notes.

'If she'd been pregnant the whole town would have known about it,' Groves said, shaking his head disparagingly.

'Why don't you think it's important?' asked the Chief Constable.

'She would obviously go to some lengths to conceal it,' Daniels said. 'A society lady—husband dead for several years—she wouldn't be exactly flaunting her pregnancy. And when it was born—I don't imagine she was anxious to launch her deformed bastard—even into what passes for high society in this county.'

If the Chief Constable took this as a dig at his own liking for the company of the local landowners he showed no reaction. Groves, however, was frowning.

'She did travel a fair bit,' he said, hesitantly.

'The boy ran away from the sanatorium in nineteen-fifty-eight,' Daniels went on. 'That was also the year Lady Bennett let the last of the domestic staff go. It was also the year she had those builders on the island, the ones who were drowned.'

He glanced quickly at their faces. The Chief Constable was still waiting for him to come to the point—but Alf was beginning to get it. That frown was un-mistakable.

'When I went to see the old boatman, Len World, he kept talking about three murders. I thought he was rambling, I couldn't get it into his head we didn't know then what had happened to Lady Bennett. But he was definite, three murders. I think he meant the builders. I wasn't on that case so I don't know how thoroughly the boat was examined but—'

'The boat was a leaky old sieve,' said Groves. 'Course, it had been rolled up and down by the currents before it was recovered.'

'I think he was trying to tell me she deliberately let them start across the harbour in a boat that wasn't sea-worthy, knowing they had no experience of boats—'

'Old Broomhead, the coroner then, he couldn't have treated the Queen more bloody gently,' Groves exclaimed. 'He skated through the witnesses—'

'You're both leaving me behind,' said the Chief Constable.

'I think she wanted them drowned, sir,' said Daniels. 'Why? Well, what were they doing on the island? I—'

'It could be,' said Groves, matches rattling in the box as he fumbled to light a cigarette. 'A place for the boy, is that what you think?'

'Yes,' said Daniels. Just at that moment he felt a great surge of warmth towards Groves. 'When we went through the castle we found a cupboard, locked, it contained forty-seven tins of stewed meats, grills, baked beans with sausages, and quite a lot of tins of pet-food. We know the old lady had her groceries delivered fairly regularly by Greeno. It's been at the back of my mind ever since—why such a big store—and why was the cupboard locked?'

The Chief Constable shook his head. Groves was nodding excitedly.

'The only answer I can see, sir, is that Richard Cavendish Smith has been on that island since nineteen-fifty-eight. I'm pretty sure he killed Greeno and Sergeant Gould and I'm pretty sure he's out there right now.'

'But you searched the whole—'

'He's right, sir!' Groves got to his feet. He was so excited he took the cigarette out of his mouth. So excited, in fact, that he dug his fingers into Daniels' shoulder and growled, 'You clever bastard!'

'Well—if that's what you both think...' The Chief Constable looked puzzled for a moment. 'We can get wheels in motion right away, eh?'

'First light, that's what we'll aim for, sir,' said Groves. 'He can't do any harm for one more night. This time we want to tear that island apart, inch by bloody inch. Eh, Victor?'

Daniels nodded. He felt drained. Why had he thought it was all so important?

CHAPTER SIXTEEN

She opened her eyes and saw a soft flame behind curved glass. For a brief moment she was a child again. It was no mere memory, she could *smell* the smoky fumes of burning paraffin. She cringed, for this was *his* cottage and she was in the little upstairs bedroom and soon *his* boots would be scraping on the stone floor of the kitchen.

She opened her eyes and saw a policeman's big blue helmet. She didn't understand that.

She tried to sit up but found herself unable to move. A spasm of nausea welled up in her throat. Wincing with a bruising pain in her stomach she turned her head to one side.

The dazzling sweep of blue feathers was only a few feet from her face.

It was a nightmare, that was all, a nightmare about Uncle Stan's cottage in Essex, the paraffin lamp, the smell, the police helmet. She moaned, twisting her head from side to side, again unable to move her arms or legs.

The feathers were still there.

Then she remembered. The bag dropping over her head. Puggy's loading bag. Puggy? Where was she? She remembered it all now, being dragged backwards over the little wall, thrown face down on the ground, still thinking it was Puggy or Julian playing stupid games, then somebody sitting on her back, pulling her hands together, tying them together, fighting for oxygen, being picked up and thrown over a shoulder, head hanging

149

down, the hard shoulder jogging into her stomach, she could still feel the bruises, the black cloth pressing on her nose and mouth. Splashing—she remembered the splashing, going through water.

Her eyes moved up the smooth sweep of peacock feathers to the dark sockets of eyes that she could not see.

Victoria screamed.

Nothing happened.

She opened her eyes again. The feathers made silken, whispering sounds as a wing slowly stretched towards her face. Something touched her forehead.

She screamed again.

She was looking at the lines on a palm, an ordinary human hand. The fingertips were tracing the outline of her temples, her nose.

The hand moved down onto her throat, the palm rubbing backwards and forwards as if savouring her warm smoothness.

She screamed again.

The fingers suddenly became rock-hard, choking her, digging into her windpipe.

'No more noise or The Keeper will have to cut out your tongue,' said a man's voice. A young man's voice. Coming from the feathered head.

The feathered shape moved. On top of its head a crown of delicate feathers vibrated in the light from the paraffin lamp, turning into a shimmering halo.

It was a nightmare. What else could it—

The hand moved back up her throat, under her chin, fingers touching her lips.

She made a desperate effort to move, to sit up and waken herself. But the pain on her skin was real. She tried again to move. Her wrists and ankles were tied!

It was a small room. The walls and ceiling were made of bare planks. Hanging from nails were strings of small white objects. Imperceptible air currents made the small white objects rotate gently with a faint tinkling sound. She stared at them unbelievingly. They were skulls, bleached, the tiny skulls of birds and rabbits and squirrels and rats. Uncle Stan had skulls like those nailed to the fence.

The hand lifted a strand of her hair.

'The Keeper likes your red hair,' said the young man's voice. She looked up. The feathered head had no beak, only a wide hole.

'Who are you? Where am I?'

'This is The Keeper's den.'

'The Keeper? Why did you bring me here?'

'Tread ye on this sacred dell the bornless keeper ye shall see pointing the road to Hell.' The young man's voice laughed. Like the voice the laughter was unnaturally precise, almost mechanical.

The feathers rustled, a gentle sound at first, like water rippling over pebbles, becoming more urgent, going on and on until the noise seemed like a thousand fine blades slicing at her skin.

Then, with one smooth movement, the feathers were pulled up almost to the ceiling and she was looking at the naked chest of a young, broad-shouldered man with a fair, unevenly stubbled beard.

All nightmares seem real at the time, she thought. The young man had the face of an aristocrat and the muscles of an athlete—but only from the waist up.

She closed her eyes and waited for the nightmare to pass, for the half-man to evaporate.

When she looked up again it was at a hard, muscly back, skin burned a deep brown. Downy hairs on his shoulders and arms made a fuzzy halo against the lamplight. He was hanging the feathered costume on a nail, carefully arranging the tail feathers so that they would not be broken.

As he moved under the light she saw the weals across his back. Old scars, so many that parts of his skin seemed corrugated.

His legs were incredibly short, thick and bowed outwards!

She twisted her head to face the bare wooden wall. A bent nail stuck out of the planking, about twelve inches above her face. Her eyes seized on it, staring desperately, concentrating her whole brain on its very ordinariness. How could this be a nightmare when she could see that nail?

She tried not to blink, fearful of losing sight of the nail for an instant.

'The Keeper is going to play tag with your friends now.'

He was squatting beside the low bed-frame. He had sun-bleached hair that hung almost to his stomach in a plait. He smiled. His teeth were brilliantly white but several were missing. His eyes were a dark brown that in shadow seemed almost black.

'Who—who are you?' she whispered.

'I am The Keeper of Peacock Island.' He smiled. 'Do you make films? I used to love the flicks.'

'The flicks?' Terrified as she was, the word made her puzzled. Nobody called them the flicks any more. 'No, television,' she said.

'Oh. Television. The Lady wouldn't have *that*.'

An arm stretched out, a powerful arm with hard muscles and a network of sinewy veins. Between finger and thumb he softly rubbed a strand of her hair.

Then he rose. He was wearing the remnant of what had been a pair of ordinary blue gym shorts. When he walked it was on the outer edge of the soles, toes turned inwards. He seemed unable to bend his legs at the knee.

'I swiped this from your friends,' he said, holding up the monk's robe. 'Nifty, isn't it?' She could see where it had been roughly slashed short so that it hung just above his thick ankles and small, rough-skinned feet.

'In the dark I'll be the invisible man,' came his voice from the cowl.

'What are you going to do?'

'It's your friends' turn now.'

'Let me go, *please*?'

'It's not a proper game if you don't have captured prisoners, is it?'

Short as he was he had to duck and walk on all-fours to get through the low mouth of what appeared to be the only entrance to the wooden chamber, a square aperture just large enough for one person to squeeze through.

She lay motionless. Then she raised her head. The floor was covered with dried grass. The policeman's helmet hung by its black strap from a nail.

Pull and wriggle as she did, until her skin burned, she could not free her wrists or ankles from the thin ropes tying her to the wooden frame. She began to scream for help.

Soon she was too exhausted even to sob.

When Maltravers raised his face out of the water the long white hull of the nearest cruiser seemed just as far away as ever, yet a quick backwards glance showed he had come at least fifty yards from the dark bulk of the island.

He took a deep breath and dropped his face into the cold water. He counted forty strokes and then looked up again.

The yacht had moved. It was now to his left.

Correcting his course he started into the breast-stroke. His arms were quite tired already. His under-pants were dragging on his hips. When they reached his knees he turned over on his back and floated until he could kick them off.

The yacht had moved again!

He decided to aim for a small cabin-cruiser whose mooring-rope he could see as a black line cutting across the lights from some windows on the shore. Through the rhythm of the churning water he thought he could hear voices, like a whispering chorus, insistent, remote.

It was water buffeting on the ears, he told himself, the same sensation he always noticed on a long jet-flight, ghostly voices singing through the whine of the engines. Then he saw Jock's lifeless face covered with brown earth.

He took in a mouthful of salt water.

Bringing his face up to spit it out he gave his arms a rest.

There was an entirely different house behind the small cabin-cruiser!

The surface was choppier now, even though his arms were not churning up the water. Little waves smacked saltily against his mouth. He felt quite weak. He trod water—and found he was still moving. He didn't have to look round to see the silhouette of the castle. It was in front of him! That was impossible.

Christ! He was caught in the current, the main channel, ten thousand acres of land-locked water decanting furiously through the narrow passage of Monks Sweep!

Behind every hero there's a naïve enthusiast like Puggy, he thought. What am I doing here? You're an idiot, Maltravers, you only jumped into the water because explaining about the currents to Puggy would have been a terrible bore.

He struck out for the large houses that lined that stretch of the inner harbour shore. The voices were louder now. His arms were very tired. It was becoming an effort to move them at all. His ears roared and cold waves battered his eyes.

As the current took him towards the last bend before Monks Sweep the lawns of the big beach houses were tantalisingly close.

Let's hope there's no cameras to record your naked arrival out of the sea, Maltravers, he said to himself. He began to push himself towards a little pebble beach.

He saw some figures standing beside an upturned dinghy. He started to shout but his ears were so full of water he could not be sure if any sound had come from his throat.

Hands touching rough stone, Puggy moved along the cottage until he came to a corner. He dropped to a crouch. The sky was a deep red, still enough light for him to see the church tower and the castle roof and the tops of trees. His ears picked up an assortment of sounds, the rustle of wind on leaves, the faint hoot of a car horn from the mainland. Was it just imagination or could he hear little squeaking sounds?

Bats!

What was the best thing to do? Wait here till Julian brought back help? Whoever had killed Jock knew this island backwards. Chasing him in the dark wasn't going to be so clever.

Was he somewhere near even now, watching and listening for a movement? Why had he killed Jock? And the boatman and the police sergeant?

And Victoria?

Oh no, not Victoria.

He had no choice. That lunatic bastard had to be kept occupied until Julian came back with the police. That was Victoria's only chance.

He ran at a crouch towards the church. Up among the trees he would be able to pick up a bit of branch or a stone.

Once he had something to hit the bastard with he would start making as much noise as possible, to draw his attention.

Then it would be a case of trying to remember what he'd been taught about unarmed combat, all those years ago at the Guards depot in Pirbright. That'll be something for the kids to tell their friends about, he thought, feeling his way up the graveyard wall.

It was the first time he'd even thought about the kids since they'd come on this stupid trip. The thought of not seeing them again made him suddenly feel quite sick.

It was dark now and the last of the small boats had gone to their moorings. The big car-ferry was on the southern bank of Monks Sweep, its lights like part of a distant fun-fair.

The iron gates clanged behind the last car to lurch up the ramp into the well between the rectangular passenger decks. The heavy links of the ferry's parallel chains rattled on concrete.

Sun-reddened people shivered in the cool night breeze. A young couple leaned heavily into each other against a rail.

As the old-fashioned ferry chugged across the racing tidal current the young lovers gazed into each other's faces.

Nobody saw the pale blob of Maltravers' face in the inky water below and nobody heard a last faint cry before he was swept past the ferry and out towards the dark expanse of silent sea.

The moment he heard the voice Puggy froze. His fingers tightened round the short length of dead branch. It wasn't much of a weapon but it was all he could find.

'Come out come out wherever you are,' sang the gleeful voice.

Puggy was at the top of the grassy slope. He could see the upper parts of the castle and the cottage roofs against the lights on the mainland.

He closed his eyes, straining to listen for the slightest sound.

'I'm coming to catch you wherever you are,' chanted the voice.

It had moved. It sounded as if it came from the other end of the castle.

Straightening up slowly, remembering an instructor telling them how the distinctive sound of cracking joints travelled at night, Puggy started to tip-toe across the grass. He heard a ship's hooter.

He heard the voice again, muffled now, probably round at the front of the castle.

He ran at a crouch for the solid blackness of the wall. Keeping his shoulder against the stone he felt his way forward, stopping at the corner, then up the side of the castle. He could see better here. He eased his leg over the low wall that ran across the castle forecourt, bringing his foot down gently, not knowing if it would touch gravel.

He flattened his back against the front of the castle. From here he could see the pathway that led between the cottages to the quay. He could see street lights and houses on the mainland.

Julian must have raised the alarm by now. If only he could keep this bastard busy.

Then he saw it, just a fraction of a second, a black silhouette moving against the light from the mainland.

He sank quickly to his knees.

'Come out come out wherever you are,' sang the chillingly boyish voice.

'I'm over here,' Puggy said calmly.

At the same time he ducked and raced for the little wall, sliding along behind it until he came to the gap where there had been gates.

Nothing happened.

Puggy raised his head slowly until he was looking over the low wall. Nothing moved in the faint light of the forecourt. Was that shadow darker than the rest? He remembered the old trick of seeing things in the dark, you didn't look directly at them, just a little to the side, it—

A heavy stone crashed against the low wall. Then another.

Puggy felt around his feet until his fingers touched something, a little clump of grass growing between flagstones. He tore it out and threw it over the wall like a grenade, reaching the front steps of the castle entrance before it landed out there in the darkness.

The next stone crunched against the wooden door behind him.

The bastard could see in the dark!

The quay! It would be light there, light enough to see, to give him a chance.

Something tripped him as he raced for the gap in the low wall.

He twisted to one side as he crashed to the ground. A black shape cut off the stars and then he felt a hard, supple body trying to pin him down, hands grappling to seize his wrists.

Puggy drew up his knees and kicked out with both feet. There was a grunt close to his face. He started to scramble to his feet. A hand grabbed his ankle. He kicked backwards with his other foot, feeling his heel connecting.

He kicked back again, his heel striking into bone and flesh. They were both breathing in rapid gasps. The hand loosened its grip on his ankle.

Like a sprinter off blocks he started to run, it didn't matter where, his very flesh desperate to escape the clutching hands.

His knees hit the low wall and he fell over it, head first. He noticed no pain. He had felt the strength in those hands. Without a weapon he would stand no chance.

All he could do was run.

His eyes seemed more accustomed to the moonlight as he pounded round the corner of the castle and made for the church. If he ran fast enough and far enough he might manage to lose himself in the trees. Julian must have reached help by now.

Against the deep purple of the far western sky he could see a gap in the treetops. That must be the path that ran along to the Roman bath.

When his foot came down in a pothole he jarred his whole body and bit his tongue. But he kept running, one hand stretched out in front in case he crashed into a tree-trunk.

He didn't know how far he had run before he stopped. He could hear nothing for the rasping noise of his own gulpings for air. He cupped his hands over his mouth, his heart thumping against his chest.

He thought he could hear running feet.

He took a deep breath. As long as that maniac was chasing him he wasn't killing Victoria. He started to run again, clenching his fists, refusing to let his aching legs drag to a standstill. If he could put enough distance between them he could look for a heavy branch or a stone, or set up a trap, if only—

Then he remembered. At the other end of the island, the little pebble beach—where Bastable the boatman was to pick them up at eleven!

He had to reach the other end of the island. With the boat he could—

There was no moonlight in the leafy tunnel of the old path and when his feet hit rough ground he had no chance to change direction or stop before a low, heavy branch smacked against his forehead.

His knees buckled as if he had been shot.

When the rapid, shuffling footsteps came past Puggy was sprawled full length in a bed of nettles, his head hanging into a long-overgrown ditch.

CHAPTER SEVENTEEN

Suddenly he was back in the small chamber, blotting out the light from the lamp. As he pulled off the monk's robe she watched with terrified eyes, cringing as far back as the ropes would allow.

He threw the robe onto the grassy floor.

'Think they're very clever, your friends, don't they?' he said. His chest was heaving. He sounded petulant.

'What—what did you . . . ?' she asked.

'Look at that!' He shoved his blond head towards her, finger pointing to a swelling under an eye. 'That was your friend,' he said indignantly. 'Kicked me in the face, rotten swine. I'll get him, though, don't worry.'

Without warning he punched her heavily on the stomach. She shut her eyes and twisted her head to the wall. Before she started to scream she heard him laughing. No more blows came. She slowly turned her head, gasping for air, going to be sick.

He was squatting a few feet away, smiling sympathetically.

'I forgot girls had no proper muscles,' he said. 'Are you hungry?'

She didn't understand. He laughed again and she started to throw up.

'Tuts tuts,' he said, towering over her as he wiped it up with a handful of grass. He smiled down at her. 'I'll have to call you Stinker,' he said. He laughed. It was the most evil sound she had ever heard. He crossed his little legs and sat beside the low bed-frame. He reached back into a corner. She saw his hand going into a mound of green moss. It came up holding a large white egg.

He cracked it on the wooden frame and then tilted back his head, swallowing yolk and white with one gulp, his lips making a slurping, sucking noise.

He wiped his mouth and chin with his hard-muscled forearm and threw the empty shell into the low tunnel.

'Don't you like eggs?' he asked, with genuine interest. 'You are the first of the nasties who's seen inside The Keeper's den. The Lady called them that, the nasty intruders. The rats ate her face off. Served her right. She said people hated me. Do you hate me? That other girl with the red hair, Iris, she wouldn't let me do it to her, she must have hated me. Do you hate me?'

His voice was too even, too precise. His facial gestures did not synchronise with his words. She stared at him.

'What are you going to do with me?' she whispered. He smiled.

'That other girl with red hair, Iris, she was very fat,' he said. 'I thought she was a smasher but she wouldn't let me do it. She said she hated me. I got my own back, though, I got her by the legs and lifted them up—woop! —and her head went down—splash!—under the water. She kicked like blazes. I didn't mean to—I was only getting my own back. Honest!' He grinned. 'You aren't fat, are you?'

His eyes moved down her body. A strong brown hand stretched out and felt for the buttons of her cardigan. His fingernails were long and a rich black.

One by one he undid her buttons, pulling the cardigan open.

When he saw the brassière he squatted nearer the bed and touched the half cups. He pulled at the connecting strap.

'Is it fastened at the back?' he asked pleasantly. 'Is it hard to run fast when you've got big bosoms?'

She couldn't speak.

He moved across the floor and reached up, his hand disappearing into the feathered costume.

She peered to see what he was doing.

He came back to the bed, thick legs doubling under his ragged gym shorts as he craned over her.

'No!'

It was a thick leather mitten held together by crude thong stitching. Protruding from the leather fist were two large metal claws.

With a quick movement a hooked edge sliced through the band of elastic. He threw aside the two half-cups and looked at her breasts, the leather mitten still in his hand.

He saw her staring at the claws. He grinned.

'Bet you couldn't make one of these,' he said. 'I got the iron bits from the old grass-mower in the stables, I sharpened them all myself on the grindstone. Like my stitches? That's like the cowboys' saddles in the flicks. Good, isn't it? Slash, slash.'

He sliced the air with the two claws, making a whistling noise with his lips. He brought the claws nearer her face, smiling at her.

His left hand took a thin twist of her hair. He severed it with one quick, slashing stroke.

He held the lock of hair up to the lamplight. He let it caress his cheek and lips. Then he looked at her naked breasts.

'You should have red hair all over,' he said, giggling.

162

He held his hand a foot or so above her breasts and slowly teased the lock between finger and thumb, hairs falling like soft leaves onto her bare skin.

'What are you doing that for?' she whispered hoarsely.

When he spoke his voice had changed its pitch, now harsher and quicker.

'Lady will have to punish you, Richard, you evil boy.'

Then, in his own voice:

'I promise I'll be good, Lady.'

He leaned over her, moaning quietly, eyes half-closed, fingers twisting in her hair, mouth closing on her nipple.

The leather mitt with the two metal claws lay lightly on her bare stomach.

The phone rang on the little table between the two camp beds. Groves snored.

Daniels reached for it. Typical of Groves, to be able to sleep. It was half past eleven. There had been no time to go home; a couple of hours on the camp beds was all they were allowing themselves before they got ready to leave for the island.

'The launch just apprehended a boatman trying to land on the island, sir,' said the radio room sergeant.

'What?'

'What is it?' Groves snapped, cutting off a particularly impressive snore.

'He's from Beckham, sir, his name's Bastable—'

'Quilt Bastable?'

'That's right, sir, the launch caught him cold in the spotlight, he says he was doing night fishing and his engine stalled.'

Daniels put his hand on the mouthpiece.

'They've collared one of our first suspects with a boat near the island. Quilt Bastable—'

'Him that got eighteen months for grievous bodily? From Beckham?'

'That's him. He says he was night-fishing and his engine stalled.'

'Was he alone?'

'Was he by himself?' Daniels said into the phone.

'Yes, sir. He does have fishing gear in the boat.'

'Bring him in,' said Groves, taking the phone out of Daniels' hand. He looked fairly ludicrous, sitting on the edge of the camp bed in his socks and underwear. He put down the phone.

'We checked that bugger, didn't we?'

'Oh yes,' said Daniels, feeling a yawn was not the right thing. 'He was playing darts in the Red Lion at Beckham on Saturday, twenty people vouched for him—'

'He'll be here in half an hour,' said Groves, shoving his stockinged feet back under the government blankets. 'I'll give him hell.'

'You don't think—'

'No. I'm betting you're right, Victor.' He snorted with amusement. 'Good job we didn't catch him last night, though.'

'Why not?'

'I was still after a thief then, wasn't I? Bastable would just have fitted me nicely. Lucky bugger. I'd have had him confessing by now. Anyway, time for another twenty minutes' kip.'

He started snoring instantaneously.

So that's why wives get aggrieved, Daniels thought, gritting his teeth against each nasal rasp from the other bed.

Eyes screwed tightly shut, teeth clenched, she held her breath as he sucked on her nipple. His hard brown body crushed down on her ribs. His hands stroked and twisted her hair.

She could not tell how long she had been here. Each second seemed to last an hour, each hour could have been one terrifying moment.

Some of the time he was cruel and violent and then he would say something that sounded like a young, innocent boy. One moment his face was pressing on her breasts, holding onto her like a child seeking comfort.

Then his body would tense with excitement and he would be pulling at her hair and clamping his teeth into her skin, his body would jerk and thrust and squirm— and then he would lie motionless, breathing heavily, not a single part of him moving.

And then he went berserk.

He had been pawing her, climbing on top of her, moaning half-formed words that seemed to be addressed to someone else, pushing his face into her stomach until she could hardly breathe, when for the first time his hands began to pull at the waistband of her slacks.

She bit her lip.

His fingers scrabbled bluntly at the press-clip fastening. He twisted violently, lying across her. She could see only his hard, brutally scarred back.

His arm rose. She saw the leather mitt.

'Oh no, please don't, please—oh no!'

She threw back her head and bit on her lip until it bled.

She felt the sharp metal tearing and slashing. Yet there was no pain. For a moment she did not breathe. When she looked again he was ripping at her slacks with the metal claws, cutting through the waistband and then down the thighs, the other hand dragging away strips of material.

He threw the leather mitt on the floor and with both hands ripped the remnants of her slacks clear of the ropes that held her ankles.

He was moaning urgently as he knelt over her. He

did not need the claws to tear her flimsy panties.

His eyes moved up and down the whole length of her body. His long plait fell onto her knees as he started to push his gym shorts down his thick legs.

Kicking them off behind, he climbed on top of her.

Puggy walked normally for a few yards, then his head span and he lurched to the ground as if drunk. He knew it was concussion but knowing didn't give him control over himself.

When he came round his arm was stiff from being pressed under his body. He had no idea how long he had been unconscious.

He staggered to his feet again and walked straight into a jagged bush.

For a time he was convinced that Julian was walking beside him, talking about what he could not distinguish.

When the concussion finally wore off he was on high ground, looking across the dark water to the ring of light on Mundham's quays. His body ached in many places.

'Julian?' he said.

Then he remembered that Julian had swum for help. The boatman! He had to get to the other end of the island. But where was he now?

If that was Mundham over there he was facing north, therefore he had to go to his left.

He walked as quickly as he could without crashing into trees or bushes, trying to picture the island's geography from what he had seen during the day. A humming noise in his ears made it impossible to hear if he was being followed.

If that maniac jumped him now he knew he stood no chance. But he had to keep going. It was Victoria's only hope.

Then he was sick. His head hung hopelessly as his stomach threw up.

'What is it?' he demanded furiously.

'What do you mean?' Her voice was only a whimper.

'I said what is it!'

He had been propping himself on his elbows, looking at her face and breasts, writhing and bumping against her.

He pulled his squat legs to a kneeling position, one hand shaking her head by the hair. He hit her on the cheek with his open palm.

'What is it you do?' he screamed, bringing his hand to rap her brutally with his knuckles.

'Oh God, no, don't! Please!'

'You're going to tell me this time,' he snarled in her ear, taking a handful of hair and twisting it until she thought it was being torn from her scalp. She began to scream. He threw her head back on the bed.

When her eyes opened again he was squatting on his haunches, a new expression on his face, the resigned look of someone who feels sad at what he must do.

His right hand was slipping into the leather mitten.

'What are you doing?' she whispered desperately.

'It's no good,' he said, shaking his head regretfully. 'What is your monicker, by the way?'

'My name? Victoria. What is it you want to know? *Please* tell me.'

'It's no good for Richard. The Lady said they would hang me, you know—for lifting Iris's legs? Iris had red hair, did I tell you? She was fatter than you. You're like the Lady, she was fat in the same places as you.'

'Lady Bennett?'

'Victoria,' he said. His brown eyes were sorrowful. 'Were you named after the Queen? You must be older than the Lady—no, you're not nearly as old as her.'

He leaned forward and with a quick slash cut off a thick strand of her hair. He held it up to the lamp, letting it brush against his face.

'They'll punish you in the most awful way,' he said in that other, harsher voice. 'Richard must become The Keeper. Nobody will find Richard on the island.'

She watched him carefully curl the thick strand of red hair, *her* hair, round and round his finger.

'Poor Victoria,' he said, in his own, soft voice.

'Was Lady Bennett your mother? The Lady?' she said quickly. 'Wasn't she nice to you?'

'She was horrid, she sent me to a place where they put things on my head and gave me pains. She had a cane, when I was naughty.'

The weal scars on his back.

For the first time she didn't feel paralysed with fear. He looked so sad.

'You've been on this island for a long time, haven't you?' she said, unconsciously adopting the tone she used for children.

'The Lady said I would be safe here. You see, I'm not normal, she explained it all to me so don't be embarrassed, I'm not like other people, I have these ugly legs and they would shut me up in places.' He smiled. 'Of course The Keeper is only a game, you realise that, don't you? It's a silly old fairy-tale, but—I didn't *actually* have anyone else to play with...'

His face contorted into a grimace. Tears ran down into the soft stubble of his cheeks. He sobbed violently, rocking on his knees. His chin was on his chest when he said, in that same unnaturally precise voice:

'You are a nasty intruder. The Keeper must punish you like the others.'

'Now listen to me, Richard, I'm not going to—'

But he was paying no attention to her as he stood up on his pathetically strong little legs. He had stopped sobbing. He looked at her carefully.

The strange thing was, she now knew he was going to kill her but she didn't feel any sense of panic.

'I know what you wanted to know, Richard,' she said calmly, 'I'm not like the others, like Iris or the Lady. I'm Victoria, it's very easy, I'll show you what to do, Richard, you couldn't do it before because my legs are tied together, you untie the ropes and Victoria will show you, Richard, there's a good boy.'

He stared at her blankly. The metal claws hung by his side.

'Come on, you want to do it, don't you, untie the ropes, Victoria won't be nasty to you, Richard.'

He moved abruptly, saying nothing. The metal cut through the thin ropes that held her crossed ankles to the bed-frame. She grimaced with the agony of pins and needles as she carefully eased her legs apart.

'Now my wrists, Richard,' she said. 'Come on, be a sport, you want to do it, don't you? I must have my hands free to show you, Richard.'

He loomed over her face, cutting one rope and then the other. She winced as the blood returned. He watched her suspiciously.

'Throw that thing down and come here,' she said, looking at the leather mitten.

He took it off slowly, placing it on the grassy floor, too far for her to reach.

She swallowed hard. Her mouth was dry. She tried to smile.

'Now, come down here, Richard, that's right, lie down beside Victoria...'

'So you weren't landing on the island?' Groves said mockingly.

'No, I told you, I was goin' night-fishin' off Dongould

rocks,' Bastable said, standing in front of the desks in the small office.

'Oh yes. You usually creep about the harbour at night with no lights?' Daniels snapped. He was playing the heavy partner.

'I don't normally bother wi' lights, I can see everythin'.'

'And you just stalled where our launch found you?' Groves said pleasantly.

'No, I told you that, I stalled an' the boat drifted that way, I was tryin' to get her started again.'

'You were coming from Beckham, you claim?' Daniels barked.

'Course I was, from my own moorin's at the old army jetty.'

'And you just drifted towards the island?'

Bastable hesitated.

'Well, I—'

'The tide would be going the other way,' Daniels growled to Groves.

'I might have bin past the island a bit—that's it,' Bastable exclaimed, 'it was carryin' me back that way, I was too busy wi' the engine to look much.'

'It won't do, you bastard,' Daniels snapped.

Bastable stared at him blankly. He felt confident. They couldn't charge him with trespassing, the boat hadn't touched ground. They were just trying to give him a fright, make sure all the other boatmen knew they were keeping a strict eye on the island.

They hadn't found out about that television lot.

His ninety pounds was still safe, if he just kept quiet.

CHAPTER EIGHTEEN

When Puggy reached the high mound of the pines he looked down on a limitless expanse of blackness dotted here and there by pinpoint lights which could have been from harbour buoys or farmhouse windows.

There was no way to tell if Bastable was down there with the boat. He could not even distinguish the time on his watch.

The thought of what he had to do now made him feel giddy again. He shook himself and began to walk slowly among the trees, arms crossed in front of his face like a blind person, feeling forward with each foot until his toe touched the heavy, stiff weight of Jock's body.

To find the matches he had to force his hand into pockets, fingers probing against cold, inert flesh.

When he found the box he turned and crawled away to be violently sick.

'What?' Bastable shouted. 'What'd you say?'

Groves winked at Daniels. They both knew they were only killing time until the search party mustered but it never did any harm to give the Bastables of this world a bit of a going-over.

'I think our Quilt's a little deaf,' Groves said. He smiled. 'Padded quilt ears, is it?' He laughed. 'I hear you're a bit of a character over there at Beckham, not got many real friends, though—'

'What'd you say about Greeno and Big Gould?' Bastable demanded. 'What's that got to do wi' me? It's trespassin' you think you got me on—'

'Oh. He's telling us what we want him for.'

'We want you for murder,' Daniels said quietly. He had been watching Bastable closely. He was beginning to suspect the man was cleverer than he appeared. On the face of it he *was* a likely suspect, but for the ... I hope to God I'm not wrong, he thought.

'*Murder!*'

Bastable started to rise but Groves was quickly beside him, heavy hand on his shoulder. 'Murder? You had blokes checkin' that I were playin' bloody darts—'

'Maybe you had a mate, you could've killed Greeno in the afternoon, slipped back to Beckham, played darts till the pub closed—we don't know when Gould was killed—'

Bastable started to sneer, showing his yellow teeth.

'Nah, you're jokin',' he said doubtfully, 'you got no idea who killed them two—'

'We've got you now, you bugger,' Daniels said heavily, 'shouldn't be too difficult to convince a jury, with your bloody looks.'

Even as he said it Daniels felt that same old sensation. There was no suppressing, no matter what you did. This was what the job was all about. This was what you *wanted*, no matter how much you tried to convince yourself it was only play-acting.

If he had thought for one moment that Bastable was seriously capable of the murders he would have been hitting by now. He knew that without a doubt and he felt a great sense of desolation. This was what he had been escaping from, hiding himself in this seaside backwater. There was no escaping it, no changing it.

His face was grim.

'Oh Christ,' Bastable moaned, sounding almost pitiable. He covered his face with his hands. 'I'll tell you then,' he said, 'there's four people on Peacock, I landed them just afore sun-up, they're filmin' for teevee, about the murders, I was goin' back to pick 'em up.' He growled some unintelligible oath. 'I knew I wouldn't get that bloody money!'

'What?' they said together, eyes wide, voices incredulous. 'You're joking?'

'I wish to Christ I bloody were!'

It took one phone call and a few words with the sleepy landlady of the Red Lion at Beckham to confirm the existence of the four London television people.

Daniels stared at Bastable.

The phone rang.

'I'm personally going to have you, Bastable,' Daniels said, his voice terrifyingly even.

'What the—Jesus Christ!' Groves shouted into the phone. 'Never mind that bloody ragtail—the launch says somebody has started a bloody great fire at the western end of the bloody island!'

Oooh!

The shock was indescribable. And the pain, tearing into her body.

She thought she was going to die. He was like steel.

But she didn't die and after a little while her eyes opened and her teeth relaxed their grip on her lower lip.

He was muttering something at her ear. His thumbs pressed demandingly into the soft flesh of her armpits.

Hesitantly at first, acting through sheer will-power, telling herself over and over again she was doing this to save her life, she began to coil her legs round his hard body.

She *wanted* to die but all the time she saw Jock's dead face and the metal claws and she began to move in time to the rhythm of his clumsy thrustings.

Faster and faster ... 'Ah—ah—aaaaaaah!'

For a moment it felt as if he was rending her body in

two. Then his face fell into her neck and he went limp.

She craned her neck, hoping to see where the leather mitten was lying. His blond head blocked her view of the floor. She knew she must not scream.

Tell yourself it's Julian, the desperate voice said in her head. Imagine it's Julian, make yourself imagine it's Julian...

And a strange thing happened.

It was madness, the voice kept saying, a nightmare, yet her hand was beginning to make little stroking movements against his shoulder-blade.

She squirmed a little under his weight, telling herself she *had* to do this, people would understand, she was doing it to save her life, he was a crazed lunatic, it was the only thing she could do. But her hand was making longer strokes, fingers exploring the hard ridge of his backbone, touching the rough lumps of his scarred weals.

His eyes opened. He smiled and pressed his lips against her perspiring forehead. She felt the urgency coming back to his body.

'Do it the way I show you,' she murmured as he raised himself on his elbows. It was madness, a nightmare, he would have killed her, but she was moaning and gasping as he began to move and she gripped him with lips and teeth and arms and legs...

'Don't stop, don't stop...'

The big spotlight picked out the man in underwear standing at the water's edge near the rotten piles of the old clayworks jetty.

Groves tapped the dog-handler's arm and he let the Alsatian off the lead. It bounded through the shallow water and stopped in front of the undressed man.

'Police—don't move,' Daniels shouted.

'Hurry up, for God's sake,' Puggy shouted back.

The launches moved in cautiously. Daniels and Groves and two uniformed constables were first on shore.

'Finding it a bit hot, were you?' Groves barked, a remark that was to become part of the local legend. In fact he was so angry he didn't really know what he was saying.

'I had to burn my clothes, everything was damp,' Puggy said. 'Look, it's a long story but we—'

'We know who you are,' Daniels snapped. 'Where are the others?'

'Maltravers was swimming—you mean he didn't get there?'

'Bastable told us.'

'Oh Christ!'

He told them about Jock and Victoria's disappearance and the fight he'd had with the murderer and how Julian had started to swim to the mainland, and the two detectives listened without interruption.

'And you're—?'

'Elder, Thomas Elder, I'm the camera-man.'

'Right. You know as well as I do what bloody fools you are. What company are you, anyway, BBC is it?'

'It's an independent, you wouldn't know it.'

'You'll be famous now, if there's any of you left to enjoy it. Victor, get one of the launches round the other side and look for this bugger who was swimming. Now then, Elder, you say the girl was only out of your sight for a couple of minutes? But you didn't hear anything?'

'Nothing. We ran half the length of the island.'

'Get into the other launch, then, while I think up some charges for you.'

The spotlight showing little shingle beaches and bushy slopes, the launch set off down the southern side of the island.

'You make a lot of money at your caper, I take it,'

Daniels said to Puggy, who was holding a blanket round his shoulders.

'I suppose so. I'm a freelance. I didn't want to do this job, but—'

'No wonder the programmes are a lot of crap,' Daniels said, without a trace of humour in his voice.

The spotlight picked out the fawn-coloured cliffs.

'One man strangled, one man almost certainly drowned, one woman missing, very likely lying under a bush with her throat cut—all for a bit of television?' Daniels said. 'What do people like you think about when you're planning this kind of jape?'

'You're quite right. You don't have to tell me.'

'Why didn't you decide to swim for it as well?'

'I can't swim.'

'Be bloody grateful you never learned, then,' said Groves. 'In fact I'd say you're the luckiest bugger alive in this country today—apart from the shit you're going to get all over you.'

'You think there's any chance she ...?' Puggy's voice trailed away.

'No, she's had it by now,' Groves said, 'unless he's also a sexual maniac, in which case she might still be breathing, but I wouldn't have thought it would be a great improvement on being dead, knowing what we do about this nutter.'

Spoken with the true brutality of the countryman, Daniels thought, approvingly.

'Did you notice anything about this man?' he asked.

'I never got a look at him—very strong hands—he seemed very small, I don't know why—'

'Because he's a bloody dwarf, that's why,' said Groves.

'You know who he is, then?'

'Oh yeah. But where's he hiding? The castle, I think, Victor, we'll have to tear that old monstrosity apart stone by bloody stone.'

As they landed at the castle quay they could see the spotlight of the other launch searching the harbour edges, but by then Maltravers was miles from shore.

'Don't stop—don't stop!'
She kissed the fingers that had killed Jock. Her legs gripped him and she wanted to laugh and scream for it was a mad dream and nothing was real and she wanted those brutal hands to bruise and squeeze every inch of her body.

It took them an hour to know there was no concealed hiding-place in or under the castle. By now the main party of dogs and constables had landed and men moved everywhere in the brilliant light of the arc lamps.

They checked the cottages and church and found nothing. In mounting desperation Daniels even opened the vault under the marble warrior again, thinking there might be a false bottom to the stone grave.

'All right, we'll have to search the whole island again,' Groves said.

'Be fun in the dark,' said Daniels.

'What we're looking for is a concealed hiding-place,' Groves told the assembled constables. 'On no account go crashing off on your own. No bloody heroes! Don't lose contact—even for a moment. Put the dogs on anything that moves.'

'What about this man Elder?' Daniels asked as they left the castle.

'Bring him along, he'll show us where his lot were working.'

'He looks a bit chilly in his underpants.'

'He's survived everything else, let's give pneumonia a chance.'

The dogs soon picked up trails and the silence of the woods was broken by the crackling static of the radios.

Roosting birds croaked indignantly. The wings of a barn owl beat softly through the tree-tops. Rats scurried into the overgrown ruins of the old buildings.

A constable lashed out with his baton at a large shape that came to life in his face. Hard wood hit thin bone and the roosting peacock screamed with rage as it flopped brokenly into the shrubbery.

Furry moths danced in the torch beams. Buck rabbits drummed warning signals on hard turf, sending their grazing tribes bolting for the warrens.

They found Jock Weir's body and had it taken back to the castle on a stretcher. An Alsatian killed a rabbit that started into its face.

At any spot where the dogs showed interest they probed with spades and crowbars, tearing away plants and creepers.

Daniels and Groves held the map under the torch.

'We've covered every damn inch,' Daniels said.

'Not quite.'

'I can't see any place we've missed.'

'Ah. I'll give you a clue. We saw them from the launch.'

'Just now? I don't—the cliffs?'

'It's the one place we've never covered, isn't it? Let's see if these wonder dogs have a head for heights.'

He was sleeping, left arm across her breasts, left leg across her pelvis. Such a funny little leg, and so strong. She stared at the wooden ceiling, in a dream, weightless, at peace, her arm encircling his beautiful blond head.

What was that?

For a moment she thought she had heard voices.

She raised her head. His legs did not look ugly to her now. Beyond his legs, on the grassy floor, she could see the leather mitten with the metal claws. She pulled his head close. Poor Julian, he had been so lonely all these years. They had both been so miserably lonely and afraid.

She let her head fall back, pressing her lips on his soft hair. There were no voices. This was their secret place that nobody would ever, ever know about.

CHAPTER NINETEEN

The police launch sidled in cautiously, the spotlight picking out the sheer cliff walls and the jumble of rocks below. The light moved upwards. There were about twenty men and dogs at the top of the cliff.

'I'll go out,' Daniels said, uncoiling the new white rope. 'You always say you hate heights.'

'That's only when I'm on the ground, Victor,' Groves said, taking hold of the rope. 'You don't grudge me a bit of the glory, do you?'

Daniels snorted. What a bloody man!

The rope tied round his middle, making some remark that had the constables laughing furtively, Groves began to move crab-wise into the brambles at the top of the cliff, hacking at the rougher shoots with his billhook, testing each foothold before moving a few inches nearer the edge.

The watching semi-circle of constables concentrated their torch beams on the greenery that was coming up to his knees.

When his legs sank from view he found he was on a concealed ledge, about six feet wide, waist-deep in ferns.

'He's at the very edge now,' said the launch sergeant's voice from half a dozen radios.

He craned out, leaning heavily on the rope.

'I want men at either end of these cliffs, top and bottom,' he was saying as hands reached down to help him back onto solid ground. 'A dog at each end as well. You know what it is, Victor?' He pressed Daniels' arm. There had been a time when his habit of touching had made Daniels wince. But not now. 'If you look up from the water you think you're seeing the actual top of the cliffs. But you're not! There's a bit of ground there you can't see from here or from down there. It's got to be here somewhere—look at the bloody dogs!'

Something was exciting them. They were making little mewing noises, only a triumph of training stopping them from pulling on their leashes.

'Let them wander round,' Daniels said.

Torch beams criss-crossed as the dogs nosed this way and that, the mewing noises becoming more urgent.

'Could be something buried here,' said one of the handlers.

'Buried alive, I hope,' said Groves.

'Get those crowbars and shovels busy,' said Daniels.

Groves took a radio from one of the constables.

'You lads down there in the launch, keep the light on the cliff, just at the top, shout if anything moves.'

It was much the same as drug addiction, Daniels thought, but he did not have time to feel guilty at his excitement.

A pick had just rapped on hollow stone.

Her hand smoothed the blond strands off his forehead. While he was sleeping she had untied the plait to let his beautiful golden hair flow down over his neck and shoulders.

Eyes closed, he smiled.

From above came the ring of metal on stone. They heard the sound of scraping, directly overhead.

'Where are we, anyway?' she asked, her voice dreamy and relaxed.

'Sshhh!'

He slipped off the bed. The noises became more urgent.

She watched his naked buttocks disappearing into the low entrance tunnel. Even then she was still drowsy and *pleased*.

He crawled back into the chamber.

'They've found the den,' he said, staring at her helplessly. 'The Lady said they'd never find it.' He looked frightened. 'It's the police, they've got a boat with a searchlight and dogs and lots of men. What'll they do to me, Victoria? You won't let them hang me, will you, Victoria? Nobody ever listens to me, you'll tell them, won't you, they'll listen to—'

Tell them!

She sat up, reaching for her clothes. With one arm in her cardigan sleeve she snatched at her white slacks. They fell apart, slashed to pieces.

'I'm scared, Victoria, you won't let them hurt me, will you—'

'You cut all my clothes!'

Her voice was shrill.

The dream was over and it was worse than any nightmare. Her face was twisted, her eyes glaring.

The noise of picks and crowbars battered down into the little wooden chamber. He was pulling on his tattered gym pants, his face pleading for reassurance.

She saw the leather mitten. Pulling the cardigan across her breasts she swung her legs off the low bed and reached down for it. She wanted to slash at his face with the claws, to tear open his skin, to rip his face to shreds. She must have been mad—no, she had done it to save her life, he was a maniac, vicious, a mass-murderer, everybody knew that, he made her do it, terrorised her, tried to kill her—that's what they must know.

'I love you,' he said, catching hold of her arm.

Her hand was only a few inches from the mitten. She tried to push him aside. He saw what she was reaching for.

Then his fist caught her in the breasts and his thumbs were at her windpipe and she was being battered back onto the low bed, his whole weight on top of her. He slapped her face, snarling wildly.

'You bastard. HELP! HELP!' she screamed.

He hit her again and she started to sob. He scrambled off the bed and lifted the peacock costume off its nail.

'You didn't even like me at all,' he said, his head disappearing into the feathers. 'You were cheating me, you rotten girl. I'll get even with you, don't worry.'

He sounded as if he was going to start crying, like a child.

Then the feathered shape crawled into the low tunnel.

All the radios buzzed to life.

'There's something at the top,' came the launch sergeant's voice.

'Keep the light on it!' Groves shouted.

The feathered shape came out of the little tunnel entrance concealed behind a bush. As he raised his head the glare of the launch spotlight dazzled the deepset eyes. He began to crawl into the ferns. A dog snarled and torch beams converged on the blue feathers.

He ducked and slithered to one side. A dog came running down through the ferns. As its jaws appeared above his head his hands shot up and his thumbs rammed into the soft sides of its mouth.

With a quick jerk he pulled it over his head and sent it hurling out into the glare of the spotlight, the Alsatian howling in terror as it writhed and twisted in mid-air and then hit the water with a splash.

He heard them shouting, crashing through the ferns above him. He scrambled back to the little bush that masked the tunnel entrance.

He pulled the bundle of sticks and rope from the hole and let it drop over the edge.

On the launch they saw the rope ladder falling down the cliff face and then swinging gently, the last spar a few feet above the tumbled boulders.

They saw the feathered figure climb sideways onto the ladder and then begin to clamber down the cliff face, the ladder jerking from side to side.

'He's going to try and swim for it,' the launch sergeant called.

'Keep the light on him. Let those dogs loose down there.'

'He's got a ladder,' came the launch sergeant's voice. 'The dogs will get him.'

'You lads down there, can you get along the bottom of the cliff?'

He was trapped.

Victoria came out of the tunnel entrance on her hands and knees.

'He can't go anywhere now,' she heard a man's voice shouting.

She blinked in the glare of the spotlight. She saw the two ropes dragging tightly on the edge of the drop. Her face was bleeding from a long, shallow cut across her cheek. She was wearing her cardigan and nothing else.

She crawled forward and peered over the edge.

'Don't hurt me, don't hurt me . . .'

Voices came from above and below.

With savage strokes of the metal claws she began to saw at the ropes of the ladder.

Richard Cavendish Smith stopped climbing down

when one of the ropes went slack in his hands. The spar fell sideways, leaving his feet dangling in mid-air. Hanging onto the other rope, he looked up.

'Help me, Victoria, help me—'

'HELP! HELP!' she screamed.

He swung on the rope, getting his feet against the cliff face, preparing to jump away from the side with enough force to clear the rocks. He had done it lots of times, at high tide, as a dare, against himself.

He was taking a deep breath when the other rope collapsed.

For one long, brilliantly illuminated moment the men on the launch saw the strange, feathered creature and the rope ladder falling together down the sheer cliff face, long feathers pluming up.

Then he crashed onto the stones.

'So that's him?' Groves said, peering through cigarette smoke at the lifeless figure on the stretcher.

'You heard what he called out to the woman?' Daniels asked quietly, watching the men in thigh-length waders lift the stretcher up into the launch.

'She was shouting for help—is that strange?' said Groves.

'No, what he was calling out.'

Groves took his arm.

'We got our murderer, didn't we?' he said, turning to walk along the pebbled beach, still holding Daniels' arm.

'She was in no danger, she didn't have to cut the ropes.'

'You want to charge her with something? What would it be, trespass? Helping the police too enthusiastically? Come on, Victor, I know we've been cheated out of a good trial but there's the inquest—you'll get your headlines.'

'Don't be bloody silly! I feel sorry for that poor little bastard—'

'He was in there long enough with her, wasn't he? Maybe he died a happy nutcase, we'll never know.' They walked on a few yards. 'Did you enjoy it—go on, admit it, you did. I never knew what to make of you, Victor, but if it isn't too embarrassing I'd just like to say you're a good nut.'

Daniels grimaced up at the night sky.

'I knew all along what your trouble was, Victor,' Groves went on.

'What bloody trouble?'

'They do say crime goes in cycles, so let's be hoping we get some more good murders to keep you happy.'

Groves went on laughing until cigarette smoke caught in his throat.

I hope it chokes you, Daniels thought . . .

Puggy still had the blanket round his shoulders when he climbed down into the launch at the end of the castle quay.

'She's in there,' said Daniels, nodding towards the little cabin.

Puggy stepped down under the low roof and sat on the edge of the bunk. She smiled at him weakly, a long strip of plaster covering the cut the metal claws had made across her cheek. She felt for his hand. He had to back her up during the ordeal that was to come, all the questions, the publicity, the public appearances. Puggy would make them believe anything she told him. That was the one good thing about stupid old Puggy, he would do anything she said.

'I'm glad you're all right,' he said, giving her hand a quick squeeze.

She pressed his hand and nodded bravely.

'At least I'll have something exciting to tell the kids after this trip,' he said, gently taking his hand away.

185

'I'm sorry I was such a bitch,' she murmured, endearingly. Her sad eyes spoke volumes.

'It was my fault,' Puggy said briskly. 'Pity we don't know when we're being ridiculous—till it's too late.'

He stood up. She started to shake her head. He stared down at her.

'Anyway,' he said, his face bleak, 'you won't have to put up with all that nonsense any more.'

Before she could speak he turned his back and climbed out into the well of the launch. He and Daniels stood side by side watching the castle recede into the shadowy dawn light.

At least Julian had enough taste to be smiling guiltily.

Puggy could hardly believe his eyes but there he was, standing above them on the quay, wearing an immaculate white sweater and jeans that were too large for him but still Julian, unmistakably Julian.

'Good God—we were sure you'd drowned,' Puggy exclaimed.

'Sorry to disappoint everybody,' Julian drawled. Below them police and ambulance-men were lifting Victoria's stretcher into position for hoisting onto the quay.

'So what the hell happened to you?' Puggy demanded.

'It was all most peculiar, really,' Julian began.

Peculiar? No, it wasn't peculiar, Puggy thought, listening in silence, it was exactly what you might have expected, with Julian. The big cabin-cruiser had been drifting half a mile off Monks Sweep, its diesels out of action but its wealthy passengers showing no concern, the sea being calm and any excuse being good enough for a party with a difference. Their radio wasn't working, either, so having hauled the half-conscious Julian

186

out of the sea and cheerfully tried to remember those jolly old techniques for artificial respiration they'd laid him out on an interior-sprung bunk and when he'd revived they'd fitted him out with fresh togs and shoved large brandies in his hand.

'So there wasn't much else to do but sit it out until the coastguard spotted us,' Julian said. Their eyes met. Maltravers waited but Puggy's face remained expressionless.

Broad leather straps holding her to the stretcher, Victoria was raised up to the edge of the quay. Kneeling men reached down to take hold of the stretcher.

'So what the hell else was I supposed to do?' Julian demanded.

'I'm not criticising you,' Puggy said quietly. There was a lot more he might have said, but what was the use? Julian's face was red with embarrassment, which might have been satisfying if you didn't stop to think of the price other people had to pay to dent the self-confidence of guys like Julian. They would always survive and the rest of us could only look on in envy and amazement.

He held back as the stretcher-men stopped to let Julian speak to Victoria. He could not hear what they said. Then Victoria was lifted into the ambulance.

'She's had a shock but I dare say she'll get over it,' Julian said, the mocking edge back in his voice. When he spoke again his face was straight but Puggy knew beyond doubt that he was smiling, inside.

'Of course we do have some rather good film to cater for the public's morbid curiosity,' Maltravers said.

'I think I possibly got some shots of that murderous little freak dressed up in that monk's robe—remember when we were hiding up behind the castle?'

'I do! We'll make a—'

'Sorry, Julian.' Puggy allowed himself the luxury of

a slow smile. 'That's what I used to get my fire going.'

'No—not the film?'

' 'Fraid so, old boy. Every bloody can.'

It was some kind of satisfaction, but even while Julian prepared his answer Puggy knew it was not enough. Nothing he did could ever be enough to put a mark on Julian.

'Oh well,' said Maltravers, 'with no film to show for all this expense I hope Victoria doesn't have too sticky a time with the board.'

He grinned. Puggy could think of nothing to say.

CHAPTER TWENTY

The two men were standing among the pine-trees on the sacred mound at the western end of Peacock Island. It was early March and the harbour below was a leaden grey stippled with white foam.

'Yes, it was a macabre chapter in our local history,' said the man in the belted raincoat. 'Put us right on the map, though. An ill wind ... do you think these terms will interest your organisation?'

'For that kind of money we'd want a very long lease,' said the thin man in the sheepskin coat.

'The council won't be unreasonable. We have the island on trust in perpetuity, the current owner is an elderly gentleman who lives in the Bahamas, he was very keen the town should have the benefit of the island as an amenity. He's as rich as Croesus, of course.'

'We could certainly make it a high-class amenity—no holiday camps, caravan sites, nothing like that, of course.'

'Of course not.'

'A yacht marina. Chalet bungalows, water-ski-ing—how would your planning committee react to a co-development scheme, giving the town a chance to participate in the profits?'

'We're a very go-ahead council. Of course we can expect the usual opposition, the same old cranks, reactionaries, they'll moan about using public money to make profits for big London developers.'

'Oh yes, the usual publicity-seekers, bird-lovers, amateur botanists, back-to-nature freaks—hold up progress for the sake of some *flower*. We get them all the time.'

'One minor point—some of my councillors have intimated an interest in preserving the old Roman bath—'

'I'm not a vandal, Mr Blyth, I'm a developer, not a despoiler, despite what the newspapers say. Naturally we'll have to tidy the island up—but there are far too many trees anyway. No, my organisation sees this as a potential show-place.'

'Shall we start back to the castle? Quite a long walk from here.'

'Self-drive buggies, that would solve the walking problem, a good system of asphalt paths.'

They set off down through the island. Passing across Pheasant Park they saw some peacocks. Despite the grey sky and stiff breeze one was making an early-season courting display, the wind blowing his fanned tail-feathers over his head.

'Magnificent birds,' said Mr Blyth.

'Yes,' said Sir Edward non-committally, 'make a hell of a din, though. Perhaps we could give them an enclosure up here, away from the hotel.' He shook his aristocratic head. 'Amazing, isn't it, a jewel of a site like this being left all these years to a lot of birds?'

'We make progress slowly, Sir Edward.'

'Not too slowly, I hope, Mr Blyth.'

'I think I can guarantee no undue hold-ups as far as my committee is concerned, Sir Edward.'

'I think you'll find us properly grateful, Mr Blyth.'

The two men disappeared among the trees. A red squirrel scampered down an oak. Blue jays squabbled in an elm. A peacock screamed. To the human ear it sounded like a screech of rage but, for the moment, it went unheard by human ear.

> *Tread ye on this sacred dell*
> *The Bornless Keeper ye shall see*
> *Pointing the road to Hell*